PRUDENCE AND THE MIGHTY FLYNN

Dumped a week before her wedding on account of being 'boring', Prudence Stark decides to turn her humdrum world upside down and live adventurously — trying all the things she's always been too shy, too sensible or too chicken to do. She leaves her teaching job in England to fly to the great Australian outback, where she meets gorgeous cattle station owner — and commitment-phobe — Flynn Maguire. Though the chemistry between them is hot, Flynn finds Pru's new outrageous take on life unsettling — while she's intent only on having fun . . .

SARAH EVANS

PRUDENCE AND THE MIGHTY FLYNN

Complete and Unabridged

LINFORD
Leicester

First published in Great Britain in 2013

First Linford Edition
published 2016

A catalogue record for this book is available
from the British Library.

ISBN 978–1–4448–2693–7

Published by
F. A. Thorpe (Publishing)
Anstey, Leicestershire

Set by Words & Graphics Ltd.
Anstey, Leicestershire
Printed and bound in Great Britain by
T. J. International Ltd., Padstow, Cornwall

This book is printed on acid-free paper

1

Prudence noisily sucked the last drops of her Pina Colada through her candy-striped straw. Delicious. She toyed with the idea of ordering another one, but resisted. It'd spoil her run. So far she'd downed a Blue Lagoon, a Harvey Wallbanger and a Head Shrinker along with the Pina Colada. So, what to try next?

She mulled it over while feasting her eyes on the view. A tangerine sun was suspended over a sea the colour of her Blue Lagoon. Not a cloud was in sight. The beach was an endless stretch of pineapple-yellow sand trimmed with lush tropical palms. Everything was perfect.

Except for the fact she was on her own.

On her honeymoon.

Pru ran the tip of her finger round the rim of her glass and licked off the dregs.

This was not how she'd envisaged her honeymoon. Where was the shiny new wedding ring? And the dishy new husband to go with it? And where was the wild, hot, steamy sex? Huh. The only thing wild, hot and steamy was her hair, which was doing a good imitation of a Medusa's head of snakes, writhing in blithe abandon thanks to the dense humidity.

When her fiancé Dean had dumped her a week before the wedding, he'd said she was sweet.

Okay, sweet was good. She could hack that.

But then he'd followed it up by saying she was boring.

Ah. Hmm. Boring wasn't so good.

'You're a sweet girl Prudence,' he'd said, gazing deep into her eyes. It was a trick of his, that eye-gazing thing. It made a girl feel so very special.

He'd done the deep eye-gazing routine thing when they'd first met, at her cousin Angie's wedding. She'd been feeling like a dowdy wallflower, whilst looking like an over-baked meringue thanks to the hideous bridesmaid's dress. She'd been bowled over by him, touched he'd bothered to spot the shy girl underneath the fluffy beige, and he'd made her feel she was the only one who mattered in the whole wide world. Or at least at cousin Angie's wedding reception.

And he'd applied it spectacularly well when he'd asked her to marry him. He'd done the down-on-the-knee, diamond ring thing, gazing so very deeply into her eyes. It'd been the complete works.

And then every day since as she'd busily organised their wedding, not knowing the dirty rat was cheating on her behind her back with the tarty personal trainer from his gym and probably seducing her with his dark-eyed routine too.

'But sweet obviously isn't good enough,' she'd said. It had been her stepsister Katrina who'd spilled the beans about the sauna frolics and illicit

3

bench-pressing going on at the gym during Dean's so-called get-fit-and-toned-for-the-wedding sessions.

'Well,' said Dean when confronted by a hurt, wrathful Pru. 'The bottom line is, love, things have grown stale between us. It's boring. We're boring.'

'But I don't find you boring!' Comfortable, maybe, but that wasn't under discussion. And she'd still believed they had a future, that the affair was a glitch on their otherwise sunny horizon.

Dean had smiled, making his meaning clear. Terribly so.

'Oh,' Pru had faltered, finally catching up with the real issue. 'But you find me boring, right?'

He shrugged.

'And gorgeous Gail of the pneumatic abs and thigh-muscles-to-die-for has nothing to do with your change of heart?'

That'd made him wince. 'I'm sorry, Prudence . . . '

'I bet you are,' she'd said, her heart

splintering into a million and one shards with every one of them sticking into her. 'So what about the wedding?'

'Don't you worry about that,' Dean had said. 'I'll deal with everything.'

And he had, bless him.

Only later Pru found out he hadn't actually cancelled the wedding and reception at all. Oh no. Because he'd gone on and married gorgeous dumb-belle Gail instead.

When she'd tackled him about it, he asked — reasonably, with a very sincere expression — what was her problem? She'd got to keep the honeymoon destination. Which, as she pointed out — less than reasonably and with a ferocious gleam in her eye — was a fat lot of good as she was on her own.

Katrina had offered to go with her on the defunct honeymoon, but Pru was adamant.

'Thanks but no, Kat. It's time I struck out on my own. I've decided to reinvent myself, before it's too late and

I end up like a bag of Mum's split peas — dried up and on the shelf.'

'You're overreacting.'

'So? It's better than being *boring*.'

'So how are you going to reinvent yourself?'

'Quit my job, go on my pseudo honeymoon, travel on to Australia and then concentrate on being adventurous.'

'Wow,' Kat had laughed. 'I can't imagine you doing any of those things, especially the adventurous bit.'

'And why not?' Pru howled with indignation. She didn't like Kat's take on her attempt at reinvention. Was she really that boring?

'Because you're too timorous. You never go anywhere on your own. You never drink too much or do stupid things. Come off it, Pru, you don't even go braless when relaxing at home.'

'Thanks!' Pru's indignation expanded a thousandfold. 'But I never went places on my own because Dean was always with me. And I didn't drink because I was always the one doing the driving. And there was no point doing stupid things because one of us had to remain sane and it wasn't going to be Dean. And as for going without a bra, I mean, well . . . '

But she didn't have an answer to that one.

'Hey. It's no big deal,' said Kat. 'Rewind to the adventure part. What are we talking about here?'

'Maybe I'll bin my sensible cotton undies and buy frivolous, skimpy, silky G-strings,' said Pru, still smarting about the braless-thing.

'Starting small is good,' said Kat, trying to suppress a grin. 'Though will slinky underwear make much difference?'

'You bet. Especially coupled with the clothes I'm going to buy.'

'Okay. So it's clothes makeover time. Which I must say is long overdue, sis. But what else?'

Pru flashed her a hurt look. What was actually wrong with her clothes? 'Maybe

I'll dye my hair wicked colours,' she challenged.

Kat dubiously regarded her sister's curly brown mop. 'That could be an interesting step.'

'And perhaps I'll pick up a man on my honeymoon.' That would take some of the sting out of Dean's defection, and she was in desperate need of some loving.

Kat snorted. 'Now I know you're kidding. You couldn't flag down a taxi you're so shy, let alone pick up a date.'

A low hit. 'I told you,' Pru said haughtily. 'I'm reinventing myself. I'm not going to hang around here and wait for another safe bet like Dean to surface at some fusty old family gathering and waste my life for another couple of years. I want some FUN.'

'Point taken. But you be careful.'

'I'll be careful as long as it's not boring,' she'd declared.

'Oh, boy,' said Kat.

'You bet,' said Pru.

And now here she was. The new Pru

had arrived. Da-dah!

Okay, so she still had to tackle the hair and the underwear, but here she was in a bar drinking cocktails instead of diet coke — a giant step for a girl who'd been conscientiously dieting for far too many months to look good for a wedding that was never going to happen.

One more cocktail and she should have enough Dutch courage to pick up a hot date in an attempt to ease the deep ache of betrayal gnawing a massive hole in her belly.

Surely it couldn't be *that* difficult, you know, to hit on someone?

She gazed around.

Hmm. The talent around the bar wasn't too inspiring. Too tall, too short, too thin, too fat, and all in board shorts and snazzy bright shirts that did absolutely nothing for them. Or her, come to that. But it didn't matter. The night was young and Pru had her whole, long honeymoon in front of her.

Her long, empty honeymoon.

This was the pits!

Depression roared inside her and she felt the tell-tale prick of tears behind her eyelids. No! She wouldn't succumb to another bout of weepy self-pity. Dean wasn't worth it. And she deserved more. This was her honeymoon, for goodness sake. So she ordered another drink and nibbled a pretzel.

Twenty minutes and a potent Hot Flash cocktail later, Prudence saw him.

It was enough to give her another hot flash, right in the middle of her solar plexus, but this time not alcohol-induced. Oh yes, he'd do very, very nicely as a bandaid for a girl with a broken heart.

He was big and beefy and golden. Mr Hunk-of-the-Universe. Now all she had to do was pluck up the courage to vamp him.

She straightened her blouse and tweaked her sarong ready for action as The Hunk scuffed through the silky soft sand towards her. He slung himself on to the bar stool, right bang next to

Prudence. Only millimetres away. She couldn't have asked for more.

Except for a double helping of courage.

Hit by nerves, she grabbed the bar menu for protection and surreptitiously studied him from the corner of her eye. He was scrumptious. Her heart upped its tempo, racing triple time, as if she'd pelted around an Olympic stadium with a starving bear snapping at her heels, and she couldn't decide if the hyperventilating was due to The Hunk or too much alcohol after her months of diet coke. More likely, a lethal combination of the two.

The Hunk summoned the barman and ordered a double scotch on the rocks. The succinct request given, the waiter cocked an inquiring eye at Prudence, catching her on the hop.

'Oh,' she squeaked mid-drool. 'Erm?' She ducked back to the menu. 'How about a Long Slow Screw Against a Wall?' she said, not realising she was now addressing thin air because the

11

busy waiter had whisked away to pour the man's scotch.

But The Hunk had heard her. Oh yes.

'Excuse me?' he said.

'A Long Slow Screw Against a Wall,' repeated Prudence more loudly, still thinking she was addressing the bartender. She raised her head and learned her awful mistake. Her cheeks flamed, clashing horribly with her pink shirt. Grief, The Hunk must think she was trying to hit on him. Okay, as a chat-up line it took some beating, but it was totally unintentional. She wished she could shrivel up and disappear. She wasn't mentally prepared for doing this . . . this pick-up thing yet. She flapped her hand in front of her face, attempting to cool her cheeks.

The Hunk blinked. 'I'm sorry. I thought you were talking to me.'

'Quite an opening line if I was . . . I must try and remember that one . . . when picking up . . . erm . . . ' Pru nervously giggled. To her consternation it came out more of a frightened squawk. 'But I was trying to order a cocktail . . . The waiter disappeared . . . I'm so sorry . . . '

'No sweat.' He waved away her apology.

But Pru couldn't stop gabbling in her effort to hide her embarrassment. 'I didn't know there were so many cocktails. It makes choosing one rather difficult. I want to sample them all. Though not all at once . . . ' Finally she wrestled control of her tongue and gagged the waffle. 'Sorry.' Now even more embarrassed, and smiling apologetically, she resolutely resumed her study of the menu.

Her eyes skimmed the list as the mist of embarrassment slightly cleared. Along with the treacherous Slow Screw, there was the Frivolous Filly and a Bosom Caresser. Goodness. Pru sucked in a breath. Who would have thought?

She started doing a mental eeny-meeny-miny-moe, still desperately ignoring the gorgeous bloke on the bar stool. What must he think of her? A complete fruit loop? Well, she'd certainly blown her chance to pick him up by acting like a dork. In fact, Pru reckoned she should abandon all plans for a pick-up until she'd had enough cocktails not to care about the consequences. Which would probably be in the next decade or two.

'Excuse me?'

Pru raised her head.

'Let me buy you one,' said The Hunk.

She looked blank.

'A cocktail,' he said.

'Oh, no! I wasn't angling for a drink!' The old Prudence squirmed awkwardly. Let's face it, even without the slow screw incident, how could she ask for a Bosom Caresser without blushing? How could anyone come to that?

'I insist. It's my way of apologising for jumping to conclusions.' His smile had the potency of neat gin on a hot day. It knocked the socks off any cocktail and made her feel all shaken and stirred.

The old Pru was sharply elbowed out the way by the new model as Prudence thought of her rash desire for adventure. Kat reckoned she didn't have the courage; well she'd show her.

And though she'd always preferred tall, dark and handsome types like Dean, tall, blond and rugged was good too. Especially when such a fine specimen was sitting on a bar stool right smack next to her and offering to buy her a drink. And The Hunk's eyes. They were the bluest she'd ever seen, apart from Brad Pitt's, and those were only on the pages of glossy, gossip magazines. These were the real McCoy.

'I accept. Thank you,' said the new, brave Pru.

'I'd better introduce myself before we enjoy, er, a long slow screw . . . I'm Flynn Maguire.' That smile flashed again causing a slash of sexy dimples in his cheeks and deepening the laughter lines around those vivid blue eyes.

Whoa! The old Prudence rushed back to the fore. She'd been right. She couldn't do this pick-up thing. It was dead against her nature. Kat was right. Pru was far too staid and too sensible to chat up a strange bloke.

And even if she had started off spectacularly well, Pru was sure she'd never be able to carry it through to its steamy conclusion.

She was too chicken.

And he was so golden and gorgeous. Even his voice was like vintage malt whisky, smoky and smooth with the hint of a power-packed punch. Half of her wanted to scuttle back into her comfortable, safe shell and consign to hell her bravado wish for adventure.

But the other half didn't.

'And you are?' said that smoky, smooth, malt whisky voice.

The new Pru reared her head again, in spite of her misgivings. In a rush she said, 'Amaryllis' in the hope that adopting an exotic name might give her a little more courage. 'Prudence' was so boring, old-fashioned and sensible, it stymied her. She'd always felt pressured to live up to its virtuous connotations. But now was not the time to be prudent!

'Amaryllis,' she repeated with confidence, holding out her hand, hoping it wasn't shaking as much as she was inside.

Those golden mobile brows whizzed skywards. 'Really?'

Prudence tried not to squirm. 'No,' she admitted. 'But it sounds wild and exotic. And today, I'm all about the wild and exotic.'

'Oh, I see.' Though he sounded as if he didn't. 'Fine by me,' said Flynn, giving her small hand a brief clasp in his own large, work-roughened one.

Prudence was aware of his thorough once-over and sighed inwardly. There was nothing remarkable about her bobbed brown hair, brown eyes and ordinary face and body.

At least not yet.

But she had made a start transforming herself. As soon as she'd hit Bali, she'd done some impulsive shopping and discarded her sensible denim skirt for a deep gentian violet sarong and her T-shirt for a thin pink top the colour of double-strength cochineal. She'd consigned the boring, safe clothes to a dark corner of her room and had self-consciously knotted the sarong around her waist and fastened the minimum number of buttons of her top as was decent before going out to seek adventure.

Flynn's brow wrinkled. 'So, Amaryllis, just how many of those drinks have you had?' he asked. He sounded as if the wild and exotic bit was worrying him, which was crazy, because it was none of his business.

Prudence narrowed her eyes. 'What, are you my keeper or something?' she said, a sharp edge to her voice.

Flynn shrugged and fingered his empty whisky glass. 'Cool it, honey. I don't want to cramp your style.'

'Good, because I've decided to branch out and kick up the traces, and I don't want anyone hampering me.'

'Hey. It's your life.' He shrugged as if he didn't care. 'So what's it to be?'

Prudence wasn't game to ask for the Slow Screw or the Bosom Caresser. 'I think I'll try a Lawnmower, thanks.'

'Coward.' His lips curved in a lethal grin. 'Weren't you suggesting something more risqué earlier? I seem to remember you asking for a . . . '

'I've changed my mind!' she interrupted, hoping her cheeks weren't flaming again, though she was feeling so hot and flustered there was no guarantee she wasn't shining like a sun-ripened tomato doused in virgin olive oil.

Flynn chuckled. It was a pleasant laugh, low and smooth with a hint of grit. He ordered the cowardly Lawn-mower and another scotch for himself.

'At least I'm experimenting,' said Prudence, pointing scathingly at his drink and wrinkling up her nose. 'Perhaps you should be more daring and try one of these. Skip the scotch and live a little.'

'I like to know exactly what I'm getting myself into, be it a drink or anything else in life,' he said with a wry smile. 'Scotch is an honest, uncomplicated drink. Those things,' he flicked his finger at Pru's frosted glass, 'look sissy but can be lethal. I'll stick to safe, thanks very much.'

Pru gave an unladylike snort. 'Now who's the coward?'

Flynn's smile widened, but he didn't rise to the bait like she hoped he would. Shame, she found teasing far easier than seduction. She sampled her cocktail.

'Good?' he asked.

'Not bad, though I think I prefer the Pina Colada.' She concentrated on the cocktail and gradually became conscious of Flynn's unwavering gaze. What was he suddenly so fascinated about? Did she have a big smear of pineapple froth across her cheek or something? She hoped not. She wanted to impress him. She had designs on the mighty Flynn and cocktail dribbles down the chin weren't conducive to seduction.

Pru sighed and stared into the dregs of her empty glass. Ho hum. She'd always felt inadequate in the chat-up stakes. She'd never been good at the man-woman thing. Her social life had been a disaster until she'd met Dean and got into an easy rhythm of socialising with him and his friends. She wasn't a bit like her stepsister. Kat could chatter away to anyone at anytime, throwing out her wildly expressive gestures, her small hands working overtime to illustrate her sparkling conversation. Pru was always tongue-tied and gawky with strangers, unless, of course, she was dealing with a classroom of children.

Well, her time with Dean hadn't done much to prepare her for the singles scene and, as there wasn't a child in sight, she was stuck with being awkward again.

She wondered how she could improve her social skills before it was too late and then jumped as Flynn said, 'Have you eaten?'

'No.'

'You should.'

'Really? So are you inviting me?' Pru decided to try out a sexy smile because, face it, she had nothing to lose and Flynn was probably going to be her only chance at a pick-up.

She experienced a jolt of satisfaction as Flynn's eyes zoomed to her lips. She ran the tip of her tongue around them, moistening the blush-rose lipstick she'd put on earlier. She was thrilled to see his nostrils flare and eyes narrow. Maybe she wasn't too bad at this seduction lark after all.

'How old are you?' He demanded, his brows lowering ominously. 'Sixteen? Seventeen?'

Prudence stiffened. Hey, she wasn't expecting that! 'Twenty-two, though it's none of your business.'

'A mere babe.' He gave a dismissive sweep of his hand.

'A babe, maybe, but there's nothing

mere about me,' she retorted, jabbing at the air with her finger to emphasis her point.

Boring! Mere! First Dean and now Mr Hunk. What was it with these men that they thought her such a nonentity?

Flynn slid off his bar stool and towered at her side. With the toe of his boot, he drew a line in the sand. 'Walk that,' he commanded.

'Oh, really!'

'Come on, Agapanthus.'

'Amaryllis!'

'Amaryllis, sorry.' He flashed a zillion megawatt smile that didn't light his eyes. 'Humour me. Walk the line.'

'I won't.'

'Won't or can't?'

Pru huffed.

'Come on, Arum Lily.'

'Agapan . . . I mean, Amaryllis!' Damn, he had her confused now! Or was it the cocktails' fault?

'Whatever, honey. You could be called Buttercup for all I care. Walk it.'

Pru couldn't believe it. 'How rude!'

'Do it!'

She huffed again and hopped off the stool. She wasn't quite sure what happened next. She'd expected to land squarely on her feet. But somehow the ground moved. And her knees buckled. And she bit the warm white sand.

'Bother.'

A smoky, whisky smooth chuckle lapped around her, making her skin goosebump even though the air was as steamy as a Turkish bath. Strong fingers clamped around her upper arms. The very next moment she was hauled to her feet.

'Well, that went peachy, I don't think. Reckon you can make it to the line now?'

His sarcastic tone annoyed Prudence. 'No sweat. I just slipped.' She shot her nose up in the air and tried to look dignified, but the ground moved again and she lurched forward. She was only saved from nose-diving into the soft white sand once more by those iron-hard, work-callused fingers.

'I think you've had your limit of cocktails. Especially if you haven't eaten.'

The effort of standing up was making Pru's head swim. 'Rubbish. Jet lag's catching up with me. I only flew in a couple of hours ago. I'm tired, that's all. Nothing a good night's sleep won't cure.'

'Let's get you to bed, then.'

Flynn Maguire get her to bed? It was enough to make Pru's head whirl faster than an out-of-control carousel.

'Ah, yes. Bed.' She tried to flutter her eyelashes at him, but her lids suddenly felt leaden. It took a tremendous effort to keep them open. What had been in those drinks?

'Which way's your unit?'

Pru frowned. Her thoughts were swirling. Maybe it wasn't the cocktails. Maybe this man had put something in her drink. She'd warned Kat numerous times about the dangers of drinking with strangers when she'd gone pub-crawling with her student friends. And

25

what had Pru gone and done? Exactly that! Except she hadn't crawled, she'd been sitting on a bar stool. A giggle bubbled up, but she swallowed it and tried to concentrate. There hadn't been a chance he could have doctored her drink. And he didn't look like a sleaze. He was so reassuringly big and confident, his eyes kind and warm, his mouth sexy . . .

She shut her eyes for a moment, musing about that very sexy mouth.

2

The woman's legs buckled and she went down for the third time. Flynn caught her before she hit the sand and swung her up in his arms, holding her against his chest. She snuggled closer and sighed deeply.

'Hey, Amaryllis, or whatever your damn name is, wake up. Which way?'

Silence answered and it was Flynn's turn to sigh. He gazed down at the now deeply sleeping woman. 'Hey.' He shook her slightly. There was no response. She was out cold. Great. Just what he needed, a comatose woman with an outlandish alias for a name. Now there was no way he'd be able to find out who she was and where she was staying. He shifted her closer to his chest. A soft bloom of honeysuckle wafted around them. There wasn't a honeysuckle flower in sight so it had to be her perfume. Flynn inhaled again. Mmm. Nice. Fresh. Pretty. Rather like the sleeping beauty in his arms.

Another sigh escaped. There was only one thing for it; he'd have to take her back to his unit until she woke. Leaving her on the beach was unthinkable. Someone with less integrity than him might take advantage. He had to get her some place safe so she could sleep off her deadly mix of jet lag and cocktails.

With difficulty, Flynn manoeuvred the sleeping woman in his arms until he finally unlocked his unit door and laid Amaryllis on the bed. He stared down at her. Twenty-two, she'd said, but she looked more like sixteen and in need of a chaperone. Sheez, he hadn't expected to end the night babysitting!

He loosened her sarong. It fell open slightly, revealing plain white knickers, virginal and pure against the paleness of her skin and the violet of the sarong. His lips tightened. She was definitely too young and vulnerable to be out on her own. He yanked the sheet over her, partly because of the deep chill of the air-conditioned room, but also for modesty. He had no desire to be a voyeur.

Against his better judgment though, he trailed his fingers across her cheek. As she murmured incoherent words, Flynn dropped his hand. Frowning, he retreated to the bathroom and had the longest of cold showers. Tomorrow he would lecture Amaryllis, or whatever her name was, on the dangers of picking up men in bars and drinking too much alcohol. The next bloke might not be such a gentleman.

He roughly towelled himself dry and slung on a pair of boxers. Quietly he returned to the bedroom where the slight, pale woman was soundly sleeping.

Flynn lay on the bed next to the young woman, being careful not to disturb her. He resolutely shut his eyes but sleep eluded him. Her honeysuckle perfume permeated the air, drifting around him like gossamer threads of

29

enchantment. He turned on his side, away from his bed partner, but the gentle sounds of her breathing played an exquisite melody. He sighed and twisted on to his back, thumping the pillow to make it more comfortable.

'Quit moving, Kat,' Prudence mumbled in the dark, her voice husky and sleep-drugged. 'Or I'll chuck you out.'

Cat? She thought he was a pesky cat?

'Hey, Amaryllis?' He shook her shoulder. There was still a chance he could awaken her and deliver her back to her own room.

At his touch, Prudence stretched with fluid grace, like a cat herself. She then rolled over and curled up snugly, smack against Flynn's chest, so her nose was buried into his thatch of golden hair. He sucked in a breath and held it hard until his chest ached. His damp chest hair must have tickled the tip of Pru's nose because she twitched and rubbed her nose with the palm of her hand. She then rolled back the other way and spooned herself into

Flynn's body, nestling until she was comfortable.

Flynn's throat convulsed. He tried to move, but Prudence lay heavily on his arm.

'Hey, Amaryllis?' he said again. 'Wake up. Please!'

His only answer was a snore.

Flynn cursed. This was going to be one hell of a long night.

★　★　★

Pru awoke to a gold-filled room. Sun streamed in through the wooden slatted shutters, zebra-striping the walls. She scrunched shut her eyes. Strobe lighting after too many cocktails wasn't healthy on the eyeballs. She lay still and wondered about her aching head and the heavy weight on her suspiciously queasy stomach. If she didn't move, perhaps she'd begin to feel better?

It was then she became conscious of the noise. Of a sound associated with childhood. The heavy breathing of the family's ancient black labrador Zek, which had, in its last couple of years, resembled a 40-a-day, emphysemic chain-smoker.

Pru, with a precious regard for her fragile health, rolled her head to one side and cranked open one, complaining, eyelid.

Whoa!

The other eye snapped open in shock. Her mouth gaped. A Greek god with golden whiskers was huskily snoring in *her* bed, smack bang next to her. For the first time ever, she had sympathy for the three bears. Who's been sleeping my bed? Well, golly, Goldie, she certainly wanted to know.

And no wonder her stomach felt so leaden. The man's big paw was flung across it possessively. Large fingers were splayed out over her waist. Her bare waist! The loud-pink blouse she'd worn the night before had ridden up. Her violet sarong had ridden down. There wasn't much left to the imagination in the middle. Thank goodness she still had on her knickers!

But what had happened last night? What had she done? Who was this golden-haired giant? Pru mentally raked through her scrambled mind.

Nothing. Except the massive pain of a hangover.

Grief, she couldn't remember a thing and she was too panicked to think straight. She had to get this stranger — he was a stranger, right? — out of her room, and fast. She whipped her head from side to side in search of inspiration and wished she hadn't. The rapid movement made her head hurt and the room spin sideways. She sucked in a deep, steadying breath and looked again, more carefully this time. Where were her bags? Her clothes?

There was no discarded denim skirt where she'd tossed it the evening before and . . . Hold on. She was in a state, but not that bad. The room had changed colour in the night. She frowned again and noted the mahogany-brown leather luggage, the dark business suit jacket slung over a chair, men's black shoes under that same chair.

Oh, heavens, this wasn't her room!

Okay, don't panic, she admonished herself. Think and stop hyperventilating. Pru then ignored her own advice and indulged in a swift panic session that included silent screaming and mental heel drumming. After a few moments, she felt calmer.

But not much.

She nibbled her lower lip and then bit down hard. The previous night's activities were slowly coming back to her in dribs and drabs.

The trip to the waterfront bar and how excited she'd felt.

The cocktails she'd sampled and how adventurous she'd thought she was being, tasting so many different ones.

The pick-up . . .

Pru then came up with a blank.

The pick-up? Then what?

Hmm. Obviously the pick-up had worked. What a bummer she couldn't remember anything else! Except his name on the edge of her consciousness.

It was on the tip of her tongue.

Tantalisingly close . . .

It was to do with a drink. A mickey finn? No, that wasn't right. Finn was his first name. Or was it Flynn? Then it hit her: Flynn Maguire. Yep, was she good or what? Hung over or not! But it was a small victory. She was still stuck in bed with a virtual stranger. And the room was still rocking as if she was on a tiny raft in the middle of the Atlantic Ocean.

She glanced again at the masculine Sleeping Beauty. He really was a hunk even if he was snoring like old Zek. But she didn't feel up to waking him and saying 'Hi, sorry, I don't remember what we did, but I'm sure it was great, and thanks anyway!'

Pru didn't have a clue what you said to the man with whom you'd just shared a one-night stand. Was there etiquette involved? She hadn't given it much thought before because the occasion had never arrived. Now it was too late. Unless . . .

Unless she could avoid a confrontation.

Hah! Great idea.

If she was clever — and lucky — she could sneak out of his room and hot foot it to hers. She worried her bottom lip. The idea sounded brilliant in theory, though in practice it could prove a mite difficult, extricating herself from the Sun God without waking him. She would have to do it carefully.

With cautious stealth, Pru lifted the large hand from her waist. Flynn's breathing didn't falter. Phew. She moved the hand sideways. There was still no action from the sleeping man. Feeling bolder, she ever so slowly lay his hand down on the sheet and let go. There was a momentary pang of regret. The hand had felt nice and cosy and intimate . . . She gave herself a mental head slap. It was precisely because of the cosy, intimate bit that she had to get out of the room and flee.

She slid off the bed and stood, barely breathing, gazing down at the golden prone body sprawled on the rumpled sheets. She experienced an acute wave of despair because her sarong was jammed under the giant's body, snagged and twisted around his muscular, gold-fuzzed legs. Retrieving it could prove tricky. If she pulled the sarong inch by careful inch, Flynn might wake up. If she yanked it in one fast, fluid motion, Flynn might spin off the bed, thump on to the floor and then definitely wake up. And that would complicate things. And he'd probably be furious . . .

Or he might not be.

He might just want to take up from wherever they'd left off the night before! Wherever that was.

Pru sucked in her lower lip and bit down. She wished she could remember just what had happened during the night. What was the point of having adventures if you couldn't remember them? And anyway, waking up this stranger and the ensuing fuss it would cause was not on her to-do list. And that meant retrieving her sarong because no way could she leave it where it was and exit the room semi-naked. She didn't have the gumption to walk through the hotel complex wearing nothing but knickers and a see-through top.

She might be breaking out from the old Pru mould but not that much and not that quickly!

Pru decided on the slow and easy approach. Her tongue caught between her teeth, she tentatively took hold of the cloth and gave an experimental tug.

Trying to concentrate on the job in hand, Pru held her breath. Flexing her fingers, she pulled gently. The sarong began to slide slowly but surely out from underneath the sleeping Flynn. She breathed out a long, exhalation through her teeth. A little bit more . . . Pru afforded a swift glance at Flynn's face.

Sleepy blue eyes blinked back.

Then Flynn smiled a slow, deep, dead sexy smile and blinked again.

Now it was Pru's turn to blink. Yikes! She tried to smile back but her facial muscles had frozen with shock.

Flynn reached out towards her in what she could only describe as a slow, dead sexy sort of way.

And that was it. Pru panicked.

She dropped the violet fabric, grabbed her purse and ran.

★ ★ ★

Flynn blinked in surprise. The girl with the flowery name, who'd moments before been filling his dreams in the most pleasantest of ways, squeaked in horror and looked as if she'd been caught stealing candy from a kid.

The next instant, her little cottontail was scooting it across his room.

Flynn jack-knifed into a sitting position.

'Where are you going? Hey, wait!' he called.

She didn't. If anything, she moved faster.

'Hang on a moment. Not so fast . . . '
The door slammed shut.

Flynn swung his legs over the side of the bed and hit the ground running. The momentum was short lived. He catapulted forward, his left knee taking the full brunt of his weight on the floor as the sarong hog-tied his legs and decked him. Flynn cursed and untangled himself from the material before limping to the door. He yanked it open.

The morning was already hot and steamy. A slight built, almond-eyed girl dressed in the hotel's cleaning staff uniform stared at Flynn over her broom and bucket and then giggled behind her hand. Flynn pulled up short, remembering his lack of clothes. He lunged back into the room and took up the nearest thing — the violet sarong — and slung it around his hips. He dashed back out on the path, but he was too late. His dream girl had bolted and was nowhere in sight.

*   *   *

Pru sprinted along the paved walkway as if the hounds of hell were nipping her bare heels. She zipped around a corner and huddled behind a large red hibiscus bush. A sprinkler was going full bore nearby and every few seconds it drenched her with a cloud of lukewarm droplets, but she didn't care, as long as the mighty Flynn Maguire didn't find her.

As she'd suspected, he wasn't far behind her. Barefoot, he slapped past her bush. Pru clamped her hands over her mouth to stop a spurt of laughter when she saw he was wearing her sarong. In spite of the incongruity of the muscular gold torso and the androgynous garment, Flynn looked great. No, more than great. He was absolutely superb and Pru stifled a sigh. Perhaps she'd been too hasty, belting off out of his room like that. Maybe she should have stayed around to explore all the possibilities open to her.

Flynn stopped dead a few metres away and Pru held her breath as he glanced around in all directions. He was mad all right. His face was rigidly aggressive, his body taut, eyes blue-diamond hard.

Pru decided in a rush that she had done the right thing in running away. She had nothing in common with this gold, cold statue of a man. It had been sheer fluke their paths had crossed the night before. He wouldn't have looked twice at her if she hadn't been muttering to an absentee waiter about long, slow screws! She blamed Dean. She wouldn't be in this mess if Dean hadn't dumped her.

She peeked through the blood-red, blousy blooms. Flynn had gone. Good, she was getting soaked hiding here. She stood up, brushing twigs and leaves from her knees and hair, then tugged down her shirt in a totally wasted effort to cover her knickers. What she needed now was a decent shower followed by a sustaining breakfast. A big, big breakfast. She was starving.

Of course, she would have to be careful not to bump into Flynn. Pru pursed her lips. There was only one thing to do. Resurrect the boring, safe old denim skirt, shove her hair into a bun and wear dark sunnies and a big, floppy sun hat. She would defy Flynn Maguire to recognise the old mousy version of herself.

3

'You've been as touchy as the new young bull in the back paddock since getting back from your Indonesian marketing trip. Anything you want to talk about?' asked Lew, Flynn's station manager. He was lounging in the doorway of Flynn's office, regarding Flynn with a half-smile on his tanned face, his eyes watchful and wondering. 'I suppose you'd tell me if the business was in trouble?'

Flynn flung down the pen he'd been twiddling between his fingers and rolled backwards in the cracked tan leather office chair. The aged leather creaked in protest as Flynn spun it sideways and shoved his booted feet up on the desk.

'The business is fine, Lew. There're no worries in that quarter. There was a lot of interest about exporting our organic beef but they wanted some more facts and figures, which I've duly sent. It's just a matter of waiting now.'

He yawned and stretched before massaging his skull, digging his fingers deep into the aching tissue. He'd been tense for days, though it wasn't as if he was unused to the hectic pace. He always worked flat out. But since he'd been back from his trip an aching dissatisfaction simmered just below the surface.

'Now, I know what's bugging the young fella out there,' said Lew with a knowing grin as he nodded towards the direction of the bull paddock where Flynn's latest purchase was penned. 'He's eager to meet the ladies and give them something to remember him by. But what about you, boss? You meet someone sweet while away?' He snickered and shifted his loose-limbed frame to a more comfortable pose in the doorway, ready to get stuck into the teasing of his boss and old friend.

'Shut up, Lew.' Flynn wasn't going to

admit to Lew that a certain young lady was bugging him like crazy. He'd be best to forget her.

If only it was that easy.

'Well, if it isn't the business and it isn't a woman, then maybe you're going down with some virus or something?'

'I'm fine. There's nothing wrong with me. I'm in the pink of health.'

'Thought so. That's why my money's on the lady.'

Flynn propelled himself out of the chair and strolled over to the window, turning his back on his laughing station manager. The window overlooked the back paddocks. He could see the new bull pacing up and down the post and rail fence, gouging a dusty groove of dirt. Flynn knew exactly how the bull felt: grouchy and impatient. Just like him. He'd been pacing a similar path up and down his study.

It was frustration, pure and simple.

Flynn rammed his fists into the front pockets of his white drill pants and hunched his shoulders.

Frustration, thanks to a flibbertigibbet who'd cannoned into his life and just as quickly dashed out of it again. He didn't have a clue who she was or where she was from, except that she sounded like some posh English radio announcer and had probably returned to the green and pleasant lands of her Mother Country, never to be seen again. Not that he had the time or inclination to track her down to find out for sure.

But it didn't stop her from bugging him.

Big time.

Lew voice sliced through his thoughts. 'You haven't been very social since your return, boss. The boys haven't seen you at the bunkhouse on card nights, or in town. Some are commenting on it. You don't usually stay away from Jimmy's Place for this long. You can't blame jet lag after all this time, mate.'

'I've been busy.' As well as preoccupied with laughing brown eyes and full, luscious lips. He hadn't felt like socialising. He'd preferred to brood.

'You should come down to Jimmy's tonight. The place is humming at the mo.'

'Why? What's the attraction? Is he boosting his sales by employing skimpies?'

'If you'd been living on the same planet as us during these past few days, you would've heard about the new babe.'

'A babe, maybe. But there's nothing mere about me.' Flynn could hear his flower girl's tart retort as if it were only yesterday.

'Is she nice?' He asked, out of courtesy; he couldn't care less what the new barmaid was like.

'Ripper gorgeous. A blond stunner.'

The blonde bit failed to snag Flynn's interest. He was more attuned to brunettes since his night in Bali.

Lew carried on, 'She's got the male population of Ibis Springs eating out of her hand. You should come and give her a look-see yourself.'

'Hmm.' Flynn carried on regarding the pacing bull. 'Maybe.'

'Tonight? Come on. It's Friday night and the boys would appreciate an appearance.'

'No. Some other time, Lew. I'm seeing Rachel tonight.'

'Ah.'

'Now what's that supposed to mean?'

'That I'm not surprised. Ms Barracuda Burnley has been asking if you were back and what was keeping you that you were too busy to catch up with folk. Seems she's a mite worried you may have met someone nice and sweet on your travels, seeing as you haven't bothered to call her since you arrived back. She doesn't like that idea at all. In fact, I bet it was Rachel who arranged tonight's date. She wouldn't want to leave it to chance, not with you being so preoccupied and all.'

Flynn was silent.

'So am I right or am I right?'

Flynn shrugged an affirmative.

'See. Won my bet. She's one pushy lady.'

'You don't like Rachel much, do you?' Flynn regarded Lew with amused interest. It wasn't the first time Lew had taken a cheap shot at Rachel.

'She's all right as long as she stays on her side of the boundary fence.'

'And what's that supposed to mean?'

'Well, boss, if she ends up with her slippers under your bed, then you're looking for a new station manager.'

Flynn gave a dry chuckle. If he didn't know any better, he'd have said the man was protesting far too much to warrant the situation. 'You like her that much, eh? Relax, Lew. You can stay a while longer. I've no intention of saddling myself with a wife for a long time yet. If ever.'

'You might not have much say in the matter, given her organising nature.' Lew gave a twisted smile, the teasing gone. 'But I guess you know what you're doing.'

'Definitely. There'll be no woman at

Ibis Springs until I have the station just where I want it. I'm not going to jeopardise things at this late stage.'

Of course, to have the business functioning at the level he wanted might take him a few more years yet, but that didn't worry Flynn. He was in no rush to get married. He knew Rachel presumed they'd eventually marry, that she fostered the notion among their mutual acquaintances. It wasn't surprising. They had the same interests, same friends and same background. Their lifestyles fitted neatly together. But Flynn wasn't going to commit, not to Rachel, not to anyone. He'd seen what it had done to his father. Three wives and three settlements had almost destroyed the four-generation family station. Because of that, Flynn wasn't prepared to take the gamble on marriage for a long time. And if it never happened, so be it. Marriage was not his top priority. The station was.

'So, we'll see you later at Jimmy's?' Lew pushed.

'Stop hassling, Lew.'

Lew grinned. 'It's your call. You're the boss, but that new girl's a real stunner. Believe me, you'd be a fool to miss out because of Rachel, or some other fancy dame you met overseas who you'll never see again.'

'I didn't say I'd met anyone,' protested Flynn.

'And you didn't say you hadn't. See you later, boss.'

★   ★   ★

Flynn didn't feel like seeing Rachel, but he owed her. He sighed deeply and took his time getting ready, shedding his sweaty work clothes, showering and pulling on clean, age-softened jeans and a blue and white checked shirt.

He grabbed the keys to the station's old runabout and tried to psyche himself up for the evening ahead. It was well nigh impossible because of the indelible vision of cheeky dimples and laughing brown eyes burned on his brain. He tried to erase it. For goodness sake, Rachel was much more his style, with her neat, ash blonde hair and cool looks. She was uncomplicated and straightforward. No saucy remarks issued from her mouth.

He cursed and gunned the runabout towards town. The quicker he got tonight over with the better, then perhaps Rachel would leave him alone for a while so he could stew in his own frustrated juices about a girl a continent away. A girl whose name he didn't know, whose number he didn't get and whose address he didn't have the foggiest notion of. How sad was that?

Though he had no intention of going to Jimmy's Place, Flynn had to drive past it to get to Rachel's. He cruised by the rows of cars parked outside the bar. The place was buzzing like bees around a flowering lemon-scented gum. He gave a wry smile. The fellas were suckers for a pretty face. Especially if she was blonde. As for Flynn, he was off blondes. He could only think as far as a saucy brunette with laughing eyes and an unconsciously sexy giggle.

Suddenly he hit the brakes, the wheels of the utility truck fishtailing on the gravel surface. The vehicle stopped mid-road. He slammed his hand down hard on the sun-crackled steering wheel. Dammit, he wished Amaryllis would zip out of his brain and stop hanging around him like some irritating blowfly. There was no point hankering over something he couldn't have. He thought of Rachel. She was neat and down to earth. She wasn't romantic or funny, but serious and sensible. She had a good business head. She knew all about life in the North-West. If he ever needed a partner, she'd suit him fine because she was prepared to take whatever he offered in their relationship. He should be thankful for that.

But Rachel was no fun, whispered a traitorous inner voice.

And that was good too, decided

Flynn stoically. No flip, saucy remarks from her. Unlike someone he could mention.

Amaryllis! It was as if she'd stuck herself to his memory with an extra dollop of super glue.

Flynn dragged his hand through his shower-damp hair and then hit the steering wheel again, hard. He didn't want to see Rachel and he sure didn't want to be haunted by Amaryllis. There was only one thing for it. He'd go and meet the blonde bombshell and hope for salvation.

Failing that, at least his appearance at Jimmy's would appease Lew and the boys while delaying the inevitable encounter with Rachel. He did a U-turn and headed back the way he'd come.

The bar was packed wall to wall and Flynn recoiled from the pungent stench of aftershave. It hit him smack in the face as he stepped across the threshold. Obviously the boys were out to impress big time. He couldn't remember the last time he'd smelt such a cocktail of cologne. This girl must be quite something to make the men bother.

He shouldered his way through the crowd, slapping a few acquaintances on the back in greeting, sharing snatches of conversation with others, but not once breaking his stride until he reached the bar where Lew was nursing an ice-cold beer and chatting to the bar owner, Jimmy Stark.

'So where's this stunner I've heard so much about?' asked Flynn after pleasantries of weather and cricket had been swapped with the other two men.

'Over there,' said Lew with a nod of his head.

Flynn spotted a pert, peroxide-blonde pouring a beer. Let that be murdering a beer, decided Flynn, as it frothed and spilled over the sides of the straight glass.

'Not like that, love,' said Jimmy hastily, grabbing a mop and going to the rescue.

Flynn blinked and stared at the bouncy

white-blonde bob and the dangling macaw earrings swinging jauntily from small pierced ears. He marvelled at the purple spangled crop top that revealed an expanse of taut, tanned belly, and the briefness of the miniscule cyclamen pink micro skirt.

He didn't know about salvation! The girl looked sinfully gorgeous. If anyone could provide a distraction from Amaryllis, she could.

If only he could bother to dredge up some enthusiasm.

His eyes skimmed down the lithe brown legs to the girl's strappy sandals. They had shells jingling from narrow fawn straps.

Flynn did a double take. He'd seen similar sandals recently. Had taken them off her feet when he'd lain Amaryllis down on his bed. Flynn shook his head to clear the memory. Those shell shoes would be a dime a dozen. Hundreds of girls would have picked them up cheap during their package holidays in the tropical sun.

But Flynn couldn't help himself. His eyes slid back to those sandaled feet paddling about in a pool of spilt beer. Amaryllis' toenails had been a sweet candy-floss pink, he mused. These were garish orange. Shame. He preferred candy floss.

The orange-tipped toes pirouetted and tripped towards him. Still staring, Flynn watched them skid to a halt.

There was a sudden gasp.

Followed by an almighty crash.

4

Pru stopped dead. Shock jolted through her system. The full jug of beer slipped from her suddenly nerveless fingers and crashed on to the red-painted concrete floor at her feet. Beer and shattered glass flew everywhere.

'Oops. Sorry!' Pru zipped down on her haunches and began tossing shards of glass into a nearby bin. She ducked her head low so her fringe of bleached hair screened her face. She knew her face was flushed. She could feel the embarrassment radiating out of her in hot, tsunamic waves.

Flynn Maguire!

What the heck was *he* doing in Ibis Springs?

'Here, love, let me do that for you,' said Jimmy. 'We don't want you cutting yourself. You go and serve Flynn.'

No! She'd much rather slice her

fingers to smithereens than face Flynn! What if he recognised her? What if he spat chips? What if he was still mad at her for running out on him? What if he was the type of man who held a grudge and would publicly decry her?

Ah, but perhaps he wouldn't know her with her new wardrobe and Debbie Harry hairstyle.

Well, heck, Pru, there was only one way to find out, girl: stand up and brazen it out.

Pru slowly eased herself upright and forced her orange glossed lips to curve into what she hoped was a sultry, woman-of-the-world smile and stared Flynn smack in the eye. She dropped her voice several octaves and slung her weight on to one hip.

'Hi, what can I get you?' She stifled a mad desire to hysterically laugh, because Flynn was acting as if he'd been sucker-punched. His eyes shot wide open while his jaw clipped his boots. There was a long, electric moment as the air pulsed a high voltage current between them.

Yep, Pru reckoned, he'd recognised her all right. So much for the Debbie Harry look. Now what?

'My God!' spluttered Flynn. 'It is you!'

'Hi, Flynn.' It sounded lame and tame but she couldn't think what else to say. He didn't exactly seem pleased to see her. More like horror-struck. Which wasn't nice for a girl's ego.

'What the hell have you done to your hair?'

And that did nothing for her ego either!

'Oh brilliant. You sound just like my dad.' Pru planted her hands on her hips, just like Flynn remembered her doing in Bali, except now those hips were encased in a pink stretchy thing masquerading as a skirt instead of the soft cotton sarong that had moulded around her curves in delicious under-statement.

Hang on — what was that she'd just said?

'Your *dad*?' Hold on a moment! Flynn did not want to be classed along with her father, not by this woman who'd tortured his dreams.

And then Flynn got another surprise when Jimmy, who was mopping up the debris, said, 'Yeah. I said those exact same words when she walked through the door.'

'She's your daughter?' Flynn had been fantasying over Jimmy Stark's daughter? He hadn't even known Jimmy had a daughter. And she'd been right under his nose in Ibis Springs all this time while he'd been pining over what might have been and beating himself up for nothing.

'Yeah, it was the biggest surprise of my life having her turn up. Haven't seen my little Prudence for a good few years. She was a squib of nothing at twelve.'

'She's no squib now,' muttered Flynn, his eyes travelling rapidly over her svelte body. 'Not a bit.' His gaze zeroed back to her flushed face. 'But what the hell have you done to your hair, your clothes? You're barely wearing any!' In Bali, she'd looked cute and vulnerable and sweet. There was nothing remotely sweet about her now.

'Considering I was only wearing a pair of knickers the last time you saw me, I don't think you really have the right to comment on my attire,' Pru said in arctic tones.

Flynn ignored Jimmy's snort of outrage and Lew's choked laugh. He was too busy back-pedalling. The woman had a point. He wasn't in the position to comment on her choice of clothes. But then Flynn saw the teasing light sparkling in those dark brown eyes and realised she was winding him up. Well, two could play at that game.

He recovered fast and slung his own body weight on to one hip in a parody of her stance and leaned against the bar. He smiled, slow and sure. He noted her sudden wariness, the narrowing of those cute, puppy-brown eyes.

'The way I remember it, we were

going to share a Long, Slow — '

Pru bounced forward on the balls of her sandaled feet, her little shells tinkling against each other, and slapped her hand over Flynn's mouth, effectively cutting off the sentence before he could embarrass her further. He stared back at her over her hand in simmering silent challenge.

Pru cracked a nervous smile. 'No need to bore the boys,' she said quickly. Did Flynn detect a quiver of panic? She wasn't as brazen as she'd like to make out. Which was interesting. And intriguing. And definitely enticing . . .

'We're not bored, sweetheart.' Lew grinned, raising his brows at Flynn and winking. 'Far from it. Do carry on. I'm fascinated.'

'I'm sure you are,' she said repressively. 'But some things should remain private, shouldn't they Flynn.' Her appeal fell flat.

'But we're all friends here. No secrets in Ibis Springs,' said Lew, his grin broadening.

Flynn could feel his own laughter bubbling deep in his belly. His lips curved against the small hand still gagging him. He stuck his tongue out, tickling her warm palm. Pru jumped and squeaked.

'Cut it out!' she hissed.

Flynn shrugged and did it again, adding a nip with his teeth for good measure. He watched with pleasure as her skin pinked to the shade of her skirt.

'So, what's this about no clothes?' interrupted Jimmy. 'Have you been compromising my little girl?'

'Cool it, Dad,' said Pru, hastily ungluing her hand from Flynn's mouth and holding it against Jimmy's chest to prevent him doing any damage. 'It's no big deal. I had a shirt on too and I would have been wearing my sarong, but Flynn wanted to try it on. Didn't you?' She batted her glitter-enhanced eyelids at Flynn.

'You saw me!' he accused, ignoring Lew's badly muffled laughter.

'You looked very fetching. Purple suits you. You should wear it more often,' said Pru with a cocky grin.

Lew laughed again and attempted to morph it into a cough when Flynn rounded on him.

'That's a mighty bad cough you've got there, Lewis,' ground out Flynn. 'You'd best go back to the station and take something for it.'

'Hey, I'm through. Once you start using my name in full I know I'm done for,' chuckled Lew. He tossed back his beer. 'I'll check on that young bull when I get back and maybe look for some purple pyjamas. Just kidding, mate!' he added as Flynn pulled himself up to his full height. 'Though it was good to know my earlier diagnosis was correct.'

With Lew gone and Jimmy momentarily distracted serving customers, Pru and Flynn were left facing each other over the bar. Pru chewed the inside of her cheek. What would happen next? Would he fling their brief but interesting past at her? And how would she react? She didn't have long to wait.

'So,' said Flynn, leaning his elbows heavily on the bar. 'You saw me go after to you that morning? What were you doing? Hiding?'

'Something like that.' She swallowed a nervous giggle.

'Like to elaborate?'

'Not really, but a hibiscus bush came in extremely handy.'

'I can't understand why you bolted.'

'Nerves,' said Pru with honest bluntness.

'Spare me. You're not the nervous type.'

'You know nothing about me, Flynn Maguire!'

'I know you like wicked drinks and adopt crazy flower names, but I guess that's just the tip of the iceberg.'

'You've got it.' Golly, he made her sound interesting. Exciting, even. Pru liked that, but she didn't like the expectant, watchful expression on his face. It meant he wanted an explanation. Well maybe if she came clean, he'd tell her what actually went on between them during that hot and steamy Bali night because the not knowing was eating her up from inside out.

'Okay,' she said on a sigh. 'I was out of my comfort zone.' She flapped her hands around, embarrassed as she remembered. 'I didn't know who you were, where I was or what had gone on. I was hazy on the etiquette of waking up next to a strange guy. I hadn't done that sort of thing before and I decided a dignified exit was called for. Less hassle and all that.' She sucked at her lower lip, watching the storm clouds gather.

'Sheez, woman, I could have been anyone!' He spat out, slapping the counter top, making a few of the guys turn their heads in their direction. 'You're lucky to have escaped unscathed.' Anger warred with concern about her welfare and Pru flinched, hunching her shoulders.

'Sorry.'

'Sorry doesn't even come close, Amaryllis. You were in a potentially dangerous situation.'

Oh, he'd remembered her false name. That pleased her, making her feel warm and fuzzy. Cherished even. But hold on! What had he said, about escaping unscathed? Okay, buster, had they shared a one-night stand or not?

'Are you saying nothing went on between us?' she asked, terribly aware she was blushing again, that her voice was shaking. But she really needed to find out. She had to know, for her own peace of mind if nothing else.

Flynn stared at her and she squirmed. There was no way of divining what he was thinking. His face was inscrutable. Just as it had been when he'd chased after her from the bedroom in Bali. Panic fluttered in Pru's belly. So something had gone on then? The silence stretched between them and her panic ballooned.

'You really can't remember?' Flynn finally said.

'I wouldn't be asking if I remembered!' she snapped.

A smile played around his eyes. Pru felt like smacking him. She also felt like kissing him. Hey, maybe that would kickstart the old memory cells?

Flynn leaned on the bar. 'A true gentleman never kisses and tells,' he said.

Oh boy, he was thinking of the kisses too!

'We kissed?' she said, her voice squeaking, which was too uncool for words.

'Amaryllis . . . ' He sounded reproachful. 'Was it so unmemorable? I'd better brush up on my technique if that's the case.'

So they'd kissed! A shiver of something akin to a blood sugar low attacked Pru's body. He could practice his technique on her any day!

'Okay, so we kissed. Big deal,' she said in her best matter-of-fact voice while madly trying to dampen down her skittering pulse rate. 'What else?'

'Damn, so kissing is not the only technique to practice. My, I must be losing my touch.'

Pru's skin prickled with embarrassment. 'I'm sure it's not your . . . er . . . technique at fault. I think the cocktails had something to do with numbing my brain.' She added in a sudden rush, 'I honestly can't remember a thing.'

Flynn's smile widened in lazy invitation. 'I guess we could always go back for a replay, minus cocktails, of course, so this time you could remember everything . . . '

The fact Pru had been thinking the exact same thing didn't make his suggestion any easier to accept. She was still too fully entrenched in the old Prudence's character traits. She had to work up to these things. It had taken her twenty-two years to drink cocktails, wear a miniskirt and dye her hair, for crying out loud.

'Erm . . . Perhaps . . . ' she stuttered.

'You don't sound too keen, Amaryllis. That's hurtful to a man's pride.' He held his hand over his heart and adopted a hangdog expression.

'It's nothing personal,' Pru blurted out. 'I'm just not terribly hot on replays, that's all.'

'Shame.' He gave her an assessing look, his slow, sexy smile tugging at one corner of his mouth. 'Maybe I could try and persuade you?'

'No harm in trying, I suppose. I'm here for a couple more days.' She reckoned she was safe. Surely not a lot could happen in a couple of days, especially not with her dad around.

Flynn must have thought the same thing. 'Honey,' he said. 'That's not long. Don't you like Ibis Springs?'

'It's not that I don't like it, but . . . '

'You need to get back to a job?'

'No.'

'You have family commitments?'

'No.'

'A boyfriend?'

'No!'

'So what's the problem?'

'Nobody said there was a problem, Maguire, and even if there was it'd be none of your business!'

There was a heart's beat pause. 'Maybe I'll make it my business.'

'Hah, you'll get nowhere.' Pride prevented her telling him about Dean's betrayal and defection, that she was the type of girl one jilted. Being dumped practically at the altar was so pathetic and no way did she want Flynn's sympathy.

'Is that so? Don't underestimate me.' Flynn's laughter suddenly died and he went still, studying her with an unnerving intentness.

She had the uncomfortable feeling he was trying to fathom her out. And she had the even more uncomfortable feeling he'd succeed, given half a chance. Well, she wouldn't give him the chance. She'd be out of here in a jiffy if he got too close.

'Look, Flynn, do you want a drink or not? I do have other people to serve.' Her hands were back on her hips, demanding.

He shrugged, allowing her to take

control. 'Yeah, yeah, I want a drink.'

'So what's your poison?'

'Scotch-on — '

' — the-rocks.' Pru couldn't resist finishing for him. 'Still being a coward, Maguire?' she jibed. 'You don't want to try something a little more special?'

Their eyes locked. Steel blue met merry, berry brown.

'Just get the scotch and stop fooling,' said Flynn dryly. 'And get a drink for yourself while you're at it.'

'Thanks. You know, everyone is entitled to a bit of fun now and again.'

Pru polished a glass and reached up to the optics for a shot of scotch. In the mirror above the bar she caught Flynn's eyes on her.

Suddenly she wished her outfit wasn't quite so brief. She wanted to hide from his heated, questing gaze. She turned, his drink in her hand. Was it her imagination or had his eyes darkened to midnight blue? Surely it was the trick of the light. 'Your ever-so boring drink, sir,' she said with a jaunty

74

flick of her wrist.

'Everything is a bit of a lark with you, isn't it Amaryllis?' He silently toasted her with his glass and took a swig of his drink, holding it in his mouth, savouring it as he steadily watched her.

'Life's to be enjoyed to the full,' said Pru who, up until a few weeks ago had never embraced that adage, had never felt the need to push the limits — not until Dean's betrayal had slapped her in the face.

'And you get your kicks by dressing outrageously and picking up strange men in bars?' He clicked down his drink and leaned on the bar, a disapproving frown between his brows.

'And don't forget the cocktails,' said Pru, goading him. 'And anyway, you've been the only strange bloke so far . . . '

'Is that right?'

Pru didn't like the smug gleam in his eyes. 'No, I was just kidding. I pick up a different one every night, it's just that I can never remember their names.'

The gleam deepened. 'Yeah, right.

You know, I reckon all that glitter and lippy hides a sweet, old-fashioned girl.'

Pru did her hands on hips routine and glared at him. Flynn chuckled.

'You have no idea what sort of girl I am,' she said, well aware she wasn't too sure herself anymore.

'If ever you get the urge to pick up a bloke, give me a call, and we'll go for that replay. Or even try something new?' He winked suggestively.

Something new? She couldn't even remember what they'd done the first time round! 'In your dreams,' she said, if somewhat breathlessly, which blunted the impact.

'Ah, if only you knew what you do to me in my dreams, Amaryllis. You're there every night . . . '

Pru did a double take. 'Really?' Goodness, she hadn't been the only one dreaming then. Suddenly she felt hot and cold all at once, which was crazy. Nothing in her sheltered, boring life with Dean had prepared her for a man like Flynn Maguire. If only she'd had more experience she'd be able to cope with these raging feelings coursing through her. But no, she'd tried to do the right thing and wait for her wedding night. Which was probably why Gail-of-the-pneumatic-abs had appealed so much to Dean. He'd got fed up of boring, staid Pru.

Well, now so had she.

And here was Flynn.

And he was offering a second go . . .

'Oh, yes, really.' His eyes crinkled at the corners and his voice was smoky warm.

'Oh.' The breath whooshed from her lungs as Flynn looked at her. Like, really looked at her. She could feel all her insides melting into steaming mush while her outsides shivered as if coated in icicles. All he had to do was lean over a little bit further and . . .

'I thought I'd find you here, Flynn,' said a woman from somewhere out of left field. 'I've been expecting you this last hour or so.'

A cool blonde — natural, not dyed,

Pru noticed with chagrin — laid her hand on Flynn's arm and smiled with confidence at him.

For the second time that night, Pru felt like slapping someone. How dare this woman touch Flynn in that familiar way! But of course, by the look of her, she'd done it a thousand times or more before.

'Rach, darling! I didn't expect to see you here.' Flynn leaned over and kissed the woman full on the lips.

'Obviously.' The woman, Rach darling, turned and gave Pru an insincere smile while her frosty forget-me-not blue eyes gave Pru the quickest once over in history. That lightning inventory left Pru feeling dirty and inadequate. For the second time in as many minutes, she wished she'd worn something more understated, more sophisticated, but she'd left all those sort of clothes outside a charity shop when she'd arrived in Perth, just so she wouldn't be tempted to revert to the old Prudence.

'Let me introduce you to . . . ' Flynn

hesitated slightly, which was under-
standable, thought Pru. They hadn't
been formally introduced yet even
though they'd been populating each
other's dreams and discussing one-
night stand replays!

Pru held out her hand. 'Prudence
Stark, Jimmy's daughter. Nice to meet
you.'

'Rachel Burnley.'

Not nice to meet you, Pru noted. At
least the woman was honest.

'Rachel's an old friend,' said Flynn.

'Oh, what a coincidence. So am I,'
said Pru, goaded into indiscretion by
the other woman's cool disdain and
trying not to question if one night of
passion elevated someone to old friend
status. She placed her hand on Flynn's
other arm and smiled.

Rachel's expression flickered. 'Really?
I've never heard Flynn mention you.'
Her tone held enough ice to provide the
rocks for a million of Flynn's boring
scotches.

'He's never mentioned you, either,'

flashed Pru. 'But, of course, a gentleman never kisses and tells. Isn't that right, Flynn?'

Flynn's eyes twinkled. 'Sure is.'

Pru grinned back and then glanced at Rachel. The cool blonde rolled her eyes and slipped her hand in the crook of Flynn's arm.

'Quit fooling, Maguire. She's young enough to be your daughter.'

'Steady on! I'm not that much younger than Flynn,' said Pru nettled.

'Is that right?' said Rachel.

'Yes, which is why I picked him up in the first place,' said Pru recklessly, wanting to shock the other woman.

'Hey, I thought I did the picking up,' said Flynn. 'I seem to remember carrying you quite a long way to the unit.'

Her damn blush came rolling back on cue. 'Remember the kiss and tell clause!'

'Oh, that's right. I'm meant to be a gentleman.' He gave her a sly wink. 'I must remember.'

Rachel had lost any interest in their byplay. 'You ready to go, Flynn? The horses are saddled and waiting.'

'It's getting a bit late to go riding,' said Flynn. 'Do you want to leave it for another time?'

'No. It'll be fine. I've packed a picnic so we can enjoy a quiet supper by the lagoon without interruptions. Maybe we can go for a swim later, as there's a full moon tonight. We've so much to catch up on.' She smiled knowingly and Pru was left in no doubt just what Rachel intended to catch up on.

Pru inwardly gnashed her teeth, but it was crazy to feel jealous over a man whom she barely knew — okay, so she'd been intimate with him, but that didn't count as knowing him.

She wished she could go riding with him, except she'd never sat on a horse. A fat, bored, seaside donkey had been the only thing she'd ridden and that hadn't been terribly successful because the donkey had failed to move an inch. And she wished she could swim with

81

Flynn in the moonlight. That would be a romantic first.

And she wished . . .

'And, Flynn,' Rachel interrupted Pru's rapidly growing wish list. 'There's something of the utmost importance I need to discuss with you.'

'Okay, Rachel,' said Flynn, his voice bland and non-committal. 'It's your call.'

'Let's get moving, then,' said Rachel with the same efficient briskness Pru had used on her primary school kids when it was getting near to home time. 'We've wasted half the evening already.'

'Oh I don't know about that. It's been a pretty interesting night so far. You sure you don't want to stay here, have a drink and enjoy the company?'

Rachel gave Pru a swift, telling glance. 'No,' she said emphatically.

'Fine. I'll be with you in a minute, then. I'll just finish my scotch,' he said.

'I'll wait.'

Flynn picked up his glass and swirled

the contents around in thoughtful silence.

Pru snatched up a cloth and began mopping up the beer spills on the bar top. 'I hope you've got your swimming shorts with you,' she said under her breath, hoping she didn't sound as snaky as she felt. Swimming at midnight indeed! And by moonlight!

Flynn grinned. 'Why would I want those?'

Before Pru could think up an adequate response, Flynn tossed his drink back in one hit and gave her a wicked wink.

'Be seeing you, Amaryllis.' He reached over and briefly touched her cheek with his fingertips.

'In your dreams, Flynn.'

Goodness! Did she actually say that out loud? Yep, she must have because Flynn's brows skipped skywards. That cute cowboy smile tugged at the left-hand corner of his mouth again. It was such a sexy, kissable mouth, thought Pru, and it was a crying shame she couldn't remember the feel of it on hers.

'You betcha,' he said.

He slung an arm around Rachel's shoulders and headed for the door. Pru watched them leave with a mixture of emotions, the main one being regret: regret that she couldn't remember their one-night stand and regret that Flynn was off on a date with a woman who wasn't her.

5

Early next morning, Prudence was swabbing the bar room floor of Jimmy's Place with a ratty-headed mop and singing along to the radio with a hideous lack of melody.

The radio blared loudly and Pru was into the beat, wiggling her bottom along to the hip-hop music and making up a string of silly lyrics as she went along. A cough behind her made her jump two feet into the air and slosh dirty water over her feet.

'Ugh! What the . . . ' said Pru before clamping her lips together as Rachel Burnley walked straight over the sloppy streaks left by Pru's suspect mopping.

'Morning, Ms Stark,' said Rachel, in her cool, bored voice.

'Morning to you too,' said Pru, feeling daft at being caught out singing. 'But actually we're closed, so if you wouldn't mind.' She waggled her mop at the woman. 'I've got work to do.'

She slopped some more scummy water about while trying to ignore Rachel. It wasn't easy because she was standing exactly where Pru needed to mop and Pru's blood pressure zipped upwards. She blamed Rachel for the cause of her heartburn last night, seeing her leaving the bar with Flynn while Pru carried on serving endless beers, wondering what they were doing during their moonlit ride and picnic — as if she couldn't have guessed! Pru'd grown increasing cranky as the night had worn on and she felt just as cranky now.

Rachel's lips tilted into an infinitesimal smile, which failed to reach the arctic regions of her eyes.

'Don't be silly, Ms Stark, Jimmy's is always open for business.' She perched on the corner of one of the lime green formica tables and swung her booted foot back and forth with casual ease. She was dressed for riding, in tight tan jeans and white silk shirt. Her hair was bobbed and perfect, unlike Pru's bleached tragedy, which was frizzing in the humid heat of the morning.

On top of her hair disaster, Pru felt disadvantaged in her daggy clothes too. Her denims were damp and dirty from cleaning and her top was one of her dad's reject T-shirts. Over it was slashed a faded advertisement for an obscure Australian beer. The shirt had been washed and sun-dried far too many times to be considered a fashion statement, if it ever had been. It hadn't worried Pru when she'd snagged the T-shirt from the back of her dad's cupboard but now she wished she'd given a little more attention to her appearance. She reckoned at this particular moment she needed all the help she could get.

'I'll go and get Dad,' she said, keen to make her escape.

'No need. You'll do just fine.'

'Great.' With bad grace, Pru leaned heavily on the mop handle and waited.

'I'm checking Jimmy knows about the party tonight. It's open to all the locals, so if he keeps a running tab, I'll settle up with him tomorrow.'

'No problem. Check the party booking and running tab it is.' Pru vowed then and there not to drink at all, or at least buy her own. She didn't want anything from Rachel Burnley.

Except Flynn, which was totally unreasonable.

'I hope you'll be there,' said Rachel, her smile still failing to warm the ice floe in her eyes.

'I've no choice,' said Pru. 'I'll be behind the bar, giving Dad a hand. I'll be in the thick of it.'

'Good. I'll see you tonight, then. Ciao.'

As soon as Rachel left, Prudence abandoned the mopping to find Jimmy and deliver the message.

'Yeah, I knew all about it, love,' he said. 'Flynn booked it. I reckon it's an engagement party.' He rubbed his hands together and smiled. 'Should be a good knees-up.'

'Engagement?' That one, power-packed word stuck in her throat. It had nasty connotations ever since her own had spectacularly floundered on the altar of betrayal. 'Whose?'

Jimmy shot her a surprised look. 'Well, Rachel and Flynn's of course. We've been expecting it for months.'

Flynn? *Engaged*?

Pru's stomach crashed to her orange-painted toes. So the engagement was the important 'issue' he and Rachel went off to discuss during their romantic horse ride. Some discussion!

'I'm surprised Rachel didn't tell you,' said Jimmy. 'I thought girls loved sharing lovey-dovey gossip.'

'Not these two girls,' said Pru shortly. Cosy gossip was right out of the equation. Pru wouldn't have put it past Rachel to feel as jealous of Pru as Pru was of Rachel. No wonder there'd been crackling ice in the air just now. Flynn wasn't the sort of man you'd want to share in a hurry and Rachel must have sensed the electric under-currents flowing between them in the bar the night before.

She sat down heavily on one of the old steel-framed kitchen chairs. 'Bother.'

'Why?' said Jimmy, puzzled.

'Because Flynn's attached to that woman.'

'Rachel? And that's a problem? But how does it affect you? I thought you'd only recently met Flynn. That you were getting over this Dean bloke.' His brows furrowed suspiciously. 'There's nothing going on between you and Flynn, is there, Prudence? Nothing I should know about?'

That was the trouble, Pru didn't know! She couldn't flipping well remember anything. She felt as if something had happened between her and Flynn because of her body's knee-jerk reaction to him. It tingled and glowed like a neon light when around him. And every time she thought of him, her body heat rose a hundredfold. But that was all she had to go on. Not a lot. Just crazy hormones.

'No, Dad. I've no claims on Flynn,' she said and grabbed the mop before Jimmy could probe further.

As she manically finished cleaning the bar, Pru made a snap decision. No way was she going to stay for tonight's party and witness Rachel gloating over Flynn when they announced their engagement. One, Pru was allergic to engagements thanks to Dean, and two, she hated the idea of Flynn hitched to any woman, especially Rachel. No, she'd make herself scarce. She'd only intended to stay in Ibis Springs for a couple of days anyway, just to visit Jimmy.

Though Jimmy had been an absentee father while she'd been growing up, with only a sporadic postcard or phone call to keep in touch with her, he'd been a perfect bolthole for her and her bleeding heart when her wedding plans collapsed. He was far enough away to duck attention from all her well-meaning family and friends and he didn't ask awkward questions. Or not often, anyway.

But now it was time to run from the action again, this time, hopefully, with her dignity still intact.

Just.

She rummaged through the paraphernalia under the bar and found a dog-eared Greyhound bus timetable stuck between a telephone directory and fishing guide. As long as the information didn't prove too ancient, a bus was due to stop at Ibis Springs at midday. She glanced at the bar clock. She had barely an hour.

She scooted off to her bedroom — a shanty sleep-out tacked on at the back of the main building — and packed her meagre belongings into her rucksack. It took less than ten minutes as she had so little with her. She then sought Jimmy, finding him in the steamy kitchen preparing a couple of rounds of toasted cheese sandwiches.

He glanced up, sweat glistening on his brow, his face red and rosy. 'What's with the rucksack, love? You're not going hiking in this heat?' He rolled his eyes. 'You need your head examined. This is no gentle English climate. You'll be fried like a pork sausage in no time.'

'Actually, I'm leaving, Dad.' Her announcement came out more brutally than she'd intended and she was surprised to feel her throat constrict, as if she was going to cry, which was ridiculous because she wasn't emotionally close to Jimmy.

But who was she kidding?

Prudence wasn't stupid.

She knew why her throat felt tight, why her eyes were pricking, why her chest hurt.

And it wasn't because of Jimmy, but Flynn. Because she wouldn't be seeing him again.

And her reaction was totally over the top, which made her mad as well as sad.

So she blamed it on Dean, again. She

was on the rebound from his ratfink behaviour. She was entitled to feel sore. Blighted love did that to a girl and she was no exception.

'What? You're not leaving now?' Jimmy stared at her, his eyes wide, disbelieving. 'But you've only just got here, Pru. We're still catching up and getting to know each other after all these years.'

'I told you it was only going to be a fleeting visit, Dad.'

'Was it something I said? Or did? I know I can't give you much time at the moment — not that I ever have and I'm sorry about that, love, you know I am. But if you give me a chance, I'll organise some time off in the next couple of days. It's difficult to get away from here sometimes, but I will try, honest.'

His stricken face caused Pru a massive pang of guilt. 'No, Dad. It's nothing to do with you. It's simply time I moved on.'

'But I want you to stay longer,' he pleaded.

She could have retaliated and said as a child she'd always wanted him to stay longer during his fleeting visits, too. But she wasn't going to dredge up old memories and past recriminations. That was over. And so was her time at Ibis Springs. She had to move on before she suffered any more heartache, because how much could one self-respecting girl take in a month?

She steeled herself. 'I'm sorry, Dad, but I'm going. I have to.'

'But, love, at least stay until after the party. It'll be a blast.'

'I don't feel like having a blast.' Hang around and pretending she was happy for the newly engaged couple? In your dreams!

'And I could do with your help, luvvy. We'll be rushed off our feet and you handle the bar so well.'

'Well, gee, how could I resist that offer? No, sorry Dad, I'm off.' She reached over and kissed him on the cheek, her eyes filling with tears in spite of herself.

'But, Prudence!'

'Your toasted sarnies are burning, Dad.' Her voice was clogged with suppressed emotion. 'You'd better turn the grill off before they morph to charcoal. Don't come out and see me off. I hate goodbyes.'

She gave him a hug and then spun on her heels and dashed out of the hot kitchen. She avoided the bar, and took the outdoor route along the verandah to the bus stop. She sat on the bleached wooden bench, her rucksack between her feet. She mopped her eyes and blew her nose several times, trying to regain control. She'd feel better once she was on the bus, she was sure of it. She drew on her sunnies — yellow ones with red polka dots on the frames that she'd bought in Perth when she'd first arrived — and stared out at the street, trying to compose herself.

There wasn't much to meditate on: a handful of weatherboard and iron houses, along with fibro ones, one white wooden church and a neighbouring community hall painted pale green. Jimmy's Place was the general store, post office and bar all rolled into one. A few smooth, white-barked gum trees and a bunch of scrubby bushes frosted with spiky yellow flowers alleviated the starkness. The scene was nothing to rave about, but there was a wild-west quaintness about the town and in the few days Pru had been there, she'd grown to love the buildings' high facades and wide verandahs, the red dust and the smoky green eucalyptus trees with their pungent, oily scent.

A utility truck clattered by, but Pru paid it scant attention. She was too busy wiping her teary eyes again and feeling sorry for herself.

A heavy tread on the wooden verandah made the boards squeak. Someone sat down on Pru's bench, causing it to sag slightly. No doubt it was another passenger for the bus, but Prudence was too preoccupied with her bleak thoughts and soggy tissues to care.

She jumped and squawked when a whisky-smooth voice said, 'A penny for them, Amaryllis.'

Flynn! The last person she wanted to see.

She whisked her tissue out of sight and sat up straighter, squaring her small shoulders, not wanting to advertise any vulnerability. 'Morning, Flynn.' She hoped he didn't notice the teary huskiness blurring her voice.

'You were deep in thought. Want to talk about it?'

'No.' *And especially not with you!*

'I see. It's a cracker day,' remarked Flynn, stretching out his long, lean legs and crossing his dusty, booted feet at the ankles. He lounged comfortably next to her as if he had nothing better to do but shoot the breeze.

Rather than looking at Flynn and feeling weak with longing, Pru gazed upwards at the pure azure canopy. It was the shade of blue a child would choose if painting a picture of the sky. There wasn't a single cloud to mar its vast dome as it stretched towards eternity.

'It's always sunny here,' she said on a sigh. 'There hasn't been a cloudy day since I arrived. At home it's grey and dismal with constant drizzle that dampens your mood as well as your clothes.'

'Don't be fooled by this fine weather, Amaryllis. It can change with a click of the fingers from balmy sunshine into wild storms and torrential rain during the cyclone season.'

Pru pulled a face. He could have been describing Pru's past few weeks. One moment calm, her wedding looming large on the horizon, and the next thrown into a storm of confusion leaving her lost and bewildered, betrayed and hurt.

Empty.

'I can't imagine a storm here. It's so deliciously serene and peaceful,' she said, thrusting her woeful thoughts away.

'An illusion. There's nothing peaceful

about the North-West and don't you forget it. It's a harsh, uncompromising environment, made up of extremes. It can claim a life all too easily if you grow complacent. You always have to be on your guard.' He tipped back his hat and squinted his gaze upwards. 'Trouble can start with the merest whisper of cloud on the horizon and build up until all hell breaks loose. Rivers roar into life and flood the land. Trees are wrenched, roots and all, from the ground. Houses blow away, stock drown, people die . . . '

Pru shivered at his raw portrayal. She continued to stare up at the blueness above her, wondering how she would have been feeling now if the wedding had gone ahead and she was now Mrs Cameron, teaching her classroom of kids and cooking intimate dinners for two in their small suburban flat, already in a cosy, domestic routine. Well, she'd be emotionally a lot less flaky than she was now, she reckoned. She would've known exactly what was expected of her. And what to expect in return.

Which must have been why Dean thought her boring.

She tensed. Was Dean now living with Fab-Abs Gail in the flat? Was she changing all the décor after Pru had spent hours painting and wallpapering the drab flat into a light airy space? She'd spent so long planning, nesting, dreaming . . .

'You're from London?' Flynn asked, his comment bringing Pru crashing back to reality.

'Yes.' She thought of her little flat again and seethed inside. She'd found the place after sifting through hundreds of rentals. Damn Dean for spoiling her dreams. She'd been so looking forward to the home-making bit.

Flynn must have picked up her anger. 'What's bothering you so much, Amaryllis?'

She felt like laughing hysterically. How could she tell him that she'd had her dreams of a perfect marriage shattered, that on the rebound, she'd met a gorgeous guy who'd pushed all the buttons she'd never known she'd had, but that he was now going off to embark on his own version of wedded bliss?

'There's not enough time to list my woes before the bus gets here,' she said instead.

'Yeah, Jimmy just told me you're wanting to leave on the next bus.'

'Yep.'

'Why?'

'That's my business.'

'It's a rather sudden decision.'

'Not really. I never intended to stay in Ibis Springs for long. I was only really here to say hi to Dad.'

'But why the rush to go?'

'I'm not obliged to inform you or anyone else of my itinerary.' How could she tell him she was leaving because of him, because of his engagement to Rachel? He'd think her daft because they'd been fleeting, one-night lovers and nothing more. He owed Pru zilch.

'Surely you can spare us a little more

of your time?' His voice was like a sun-warmed caress and it took all Pru's willpower not to respond to it.

'The thing is, I don't feel like it.' Her voice came out strangled. Pru coughed and tried to clear the lump forming mid-throat.

Flynn sighed. 'But I was hoping to get to know you better.' He sounded regretful.

The throat lump solidified, almost choking her. How could he say that, now he was engaged and all?

'Good grief, Flynn.' Anger began to bubble in her bloodstream, drowning the sadness. He was no different from cheating rat Dean. It was one thing to flirt while single, but the rules changed once one was engaged — or they should. Pru might not like Rachel very much, but she wasn't going to expose her to the same humiliation Pru had suffered. 'You can't seriously mean that?'

He chuckled. It was warm and gravelly and gorgeous which made her all the more cross. 'I do. Stay, sweetheart.' He picked up her hand and held it snugly in his. In spite of everything, it felt good.

It felt right.

But it was wrong, wrong, *wrong*!

Prudence tugged her hand away, re-crossed her arms across her chest and stared stolidly in front of her. 'No.'

'What can I say that would persuade you?'

That you're not going to marry Rachel! As if that was going to happen on the eve of his engagement.

'Nothing. It's time to move on. I want to go.' Needed to go. Heck, she was going to cry again.

'Prudence . . . ' Flynn said softly.

With reluctance, Pru turned towards him. He calmly reached over and slid off her yellow and red sunglasses. He stared down into her eyes; eyes that she suspected were red from crying and matched the red polka dots admirably. Gently he touched the damp skin where her eyelashes tangled at the corner of her eye.

'You don't strike me as a girl who's eager to leave,' he said. His voice was low and caressing and shivered across her sensitive nerves. 'Stay.'

Pru could feel a sob rising to the surface, just like an air bubble in water. She clamped down on it before it found form and embarrassed her. She snatched her glasses from his fingers and rammed them back on her nose, which she then stuck loftily in the air. 'Leave me alone, Flynn Maguire,' she bit out. 'You might be the big boss around town, but you don't order me about.'

'I wasn't ordering, I was asking,' he said mildly.

'Same difference.'

He chuckled again. 'You chose your pseudonym poorly. You're no Amaryllis. You're more like one of our wild desert flowers; small, prickly and untamed but exquisite with it.'

Pru didn't know quite how to react to his comment. Was he complimenting her? She wasn't sure. She really hoped he wasn't. Flynn had no right hitting on her now he was engaged to Rachel Burnley.

She glanced at her watch. The bus was late. Very. It was almost one o'clock. The one moment in her life she needed a bus on time and it was running late.

'Don't you have something better to do than sit here annoying me?' she said huffily.

'Nope. Can't think of anything I'd rather be doing.'

'I can. Go and find Rachel.'

'She's busy.'

'Go and be busy with her.'

'She wouldn't thank me for it. She's getting her hair done for tonight. I'd only cramp her style.'

Grief, but he was being calm about his fiancée's preparation for their big night while flirting with another woman.

Pain twisted in her heart. Surely not all men were this deceitful? Were there any decent men out there?

Jimmy appeared on the verandah. He was looking ridiculously pleased with himself, his grin splitting almost as wide as his rosy face. 'The bus company's just called. There's a drivers' strike so there won't be any buses for the next couple of days,' he informed them with a hearty laugh. 'It means you can stay, love. Isn't that terrific?'

Pru's heart hit the dirt at speed. Not for her. Now there'd be no escaping this fiasco.

'Excellent,' said Flynn ruffling her hair as he rose to his feet. 'That means you won't miss the party. Save me a couple of dances, won't you, sweetheart.'

She scowled at him. 'But what about Rachel? She won't like that.'

'Rachel doesn't own me, my little desert flower. I'll be seeing you tonight and I'll hold you to those dances.' He dropped a kiss on top of her tousled head and sauntered away, his long legs covering the ground with primal animal grace.

Dropping her head in her hands, Pru groaned. The thought of dancing with Flynn sent deliciously sinful sensations coursing through her bloodstream but it wasn't right. She wouldn't muscle in on another woman's fiancé. She knew how much that hurt. Prudence would have to avoid him. It was the only decent thing she could do under the circumstances.

6

It was late and the party was in full swing. Pru had lost count of how many jugs of beer she'd served. The place was packed to bursting. People had turned up from miles around, not wanting to miss out on what was being touted as the celebration of the year.

Rachel had arrived early and was sitting at a far table with a group of women. Flynn was conspicuous by his absence. He wasn't acting very lover-like, Pru decided. If this had been their engagement party, she would have liked to have had him present at least, if not glued to her side.

A vision of her own and Dean's engagement party flashed in front of her. Their families and friends had been crammed into her mum and step-dad's living room, eating finger food and drinking cheap supermarket wine. She'd been on the sofa, rammed between Dean and an ancient aunt. They'd been lots of hugging and kissing and congratulations. The atmosphere had been warm and special.

This was a very different show.

It could have been any ordinary, let-your-hair-down-for-the-weekend, Friday night. There wasn't a feel of celebration, or anticipation.

In fact, it didn't feel like an engagement party at all, especially after a shout went out from a rowdy knot of station hands for the karaoke machine to be set up.

Until she'd arrived in Australia, Pru had never experienced this form of entertainment and, for all her glumness, she couldn't help laughing at the hilarious attempts of those who took turns to belt out old time favourites like *I Did It My Way* and *Don't Fence Me In*.

'Come on, Pru, you have a go,' declared one of the boys in a black akubra hat, country-and-western shirt and snug blue jeans.

'But I can't sing,' she protested.

'And we can? Come on, show us how it's done, darl.'

'No, I really can't sing.' And she meant it. Even the children in her class had realised that fact as she'd mangled nursery song after nursery song during their music sessions.

But the men wouldn't be put off. They started pounding the tables and stamping their feet, shouting for her to sing.

'Well, okay,' she capitulated, deciding it was the only way to shut them up and stop embarrassing her. 'You asked for it, but don't say I didn't warn you. What do you want me to sing?'

'*Don't Go Breaking My Heart* and I'll do Elton's part,' said a young jackaroo in a red-checked shirt and leather waistcoat. He was tall and thin with a mop of thick red hair and not a piece of bling to be seen upon his person. He was the complete antithesis of Elton John.

Pru sang with her partner and it was as terrible as she'd threatened. The place erupted in delighted laughter and the partygoers demanded more. She butchered three more songs before she begged them to let her leave the stage.

'You've humiliated me enough,' she pleaded. 'Let me go.'

'Sing *Please Release Me*!' hollered the black akubra. 'And then we'll let you go, darlin'.'

She agreed, under sufferance, and as she crucified the song, her eyes alighted on Flynn.

He was lounging against the doorjamb. He'd been there for a while, judging by the half-finished beer in his hand. A smile tugged at his lips as his eyes fixed on her.

She gave the song her best shot, which wasn't saying much considering her lack of talent, before she was lifted from the stage by the jackaroo who'd sung Elton's part.

'That was awesome,' said the young

bloke, beaming. 'I reckon us two should go on tour.'

'Oh yeah? We'd have to pay people to come and listen to us.' Pru chuckled. 'But thanks for the offer.'

Over the jackaroo's shoulder, Pru saw Flynn push himself away from the doorframe and saunter through the crowd. He looked as though he was coming straight towards her, but surely he would go to Rachel, as this was their big night?

But he didn't. He reached the bar the same time as Pru.

'That was some performance,' he said, trying unsuccessfully to keep a straight face.

'I did warn them I couldn't sing.' Her adrenaline-fired giggles bubbled over. She was on a natural high from her impromptu stage show.

'You can't expect to have it all.'

'I don't have anything! I'm the most boring person around. Miss Boringly Mediocre, that's me,' she retorted with a derisive snort. 'And I can't sing karaoke for quids.'

'Okay, I concede you're spot-on about the karaoke. But as for the boring bit, you're kidding me, right?' said Flynn, tipping her chin up with one finger and making her feel all flustered and hot.

'No. I am very aware of my limitations.' *Thanks to her cheating ex.*

'Darling Amaryllis, you have beauty, brains and the cutest bottom in the Southern Hemisphere.'

'I do?' She blinked, unable to believe what he was saying and feeling the tell-tale blush of embarrassment staining her cheeks. And she wasn't just embarrassed. She was ridiculously pleased by his comments, which annoyed her on top of it all.

'You do.'

'The cutest bottom, eh?'

'Indubitably. Now how about one of those dances you promised me?'

'Oh, but . . . ' Too late she remembered her decision not to dance with him. That she was going to avoid him the whole night.

'No buts. I've been looking forward to this all day. You can't disappoint me now.'

While she was still stuttering and spluttering excuses, Flynn slung an arm around her shoulder and steered her firmly towards the small area of floor cleared for dancing. He drew her into the circle of his arms and held her tight against his lean body.

Pru abruptly stopped stuttering, too swamped by the intense impact his long, hard frame was having on her. Though her head told her she should duck out of his embrace and make a run for it, her heart wanted the opposite.

In a rush, Pru decided she had no choice but to shut her eyes and relish the feel of him because it would be the only chance she'd get to have his arms closed tight around her, for her to enjoy his musky male scent, feel his warmth and strength.

She could enjoy him for this one dance.

Because after that, he was all Rachel's.

Or, at least, that's what she told herself as she melted into his arms and gave herself over to the music.

★ ★ ★

Flynn rested his chin on the top of the silky blonde head. It was good to have Amaryllis back in his arms. He'd wanted to hold her for the longest time. And she felt so right, snuggled close to him with her enchanting honeysuckle scent weaving its subtle magic around them.

It transported him back to that first night in Bali, when she'd slept so sweetly and deeply next to him. Just the memory made his blood rush through his body with a keening need bordering on desperation.

She'd looked so darned hot on stage. She'd shaken her head along to the beat, swinging her crazy mop of bleached hair, and wiggling her hips.

But she still exuded the same air of innocence she'd had in Bali. What an intriguing package she was.

'One dance and that's it,' said Pru, cutting through his thoughts.

'Why the rationing?' he drawled with a smile. 'We can dance all night if we want, which would suit me just fine, by the way.'

'Oh, come on, Flynn. I don't think so.'

'I do.'

'Don't you think you should consider Rachel?'

'No.' He tried to snuggle her closer but he felt definite resistance. Damn but she was full of inconsistencies.

They danced in silence for a few moments. Gradually he felt her relax back against him. Now this was more like it . . . He let his lips play across her silky hair. Immediately her body stiffened again. Flynn inwardly sighed.

'Don't,' she hissed. 'Or I quit dancing.'

'Hey, why so uptight? You weren't

117

like this in Bali.'

'This isn't Bali.'

'No, but while the venue's changed, you and I are the same.'

'No, we're not.'

Flynn was surprised how adamant she was.

'Nothing's changed, Amaryllis.' Except he now knew her name and where she came from. And that now she was so embedded in his psyche he wanted her with a deep aching need that refused to go away.

'I've changed,' she said abruptly, arching away from him further so she could dodge his caress.

'How so, apart from the crazy hair and clothes?' He watched her nibble her bottom lip as if she was debating what to divulge.

'I'm not going to bore you with the details.'

'I promise you, I won't be bored. I don't think you could ever bore me. You're one of the most intriguing women I've ever met.'

Pru rolled her eyes as if she didn't believe him and then said, 'Okay. You're no longer a stranger.'

'Surely that's a plus, babe?'

'Not in my book. It's one thing picking up a complete stranger and flirting with him until kingdom come, but I know who you are now and all the baggage that comes with that knowledge.'

'Baggage?' He frowned. What was she going on about? 'What sort of, er . . . baggage?'

'You and Rachel-type baggage.'

'I don't think Rachel would like to be tagged as baggage.' He chuckled. 'She'd consider the label far beneath her. A Burnley stands for something in these parts. The family's a big noise, not some stray piece of luggage.'

'You know what I mean. Your relationship with her.'

'Rach and I go back a long way, if that's what you mean.'

'That's right, you do. You've got history together. As for you and me, we don't.'

'You're being illogical. I've known Rachel since we were kids. You and I have only just met. We can't change those facts.'

'Don't I know it.' She suddenly sounded so incredibly sad that Flynn gathered her closer, tucking her more snugly against his body.

'But there's nothing to stop us getting to know each other better. Nothing at all. I for one would welcome the opportunity.'

'Hmm.' She didn't sound convinced.

'And we can start with these changes you mentioned . . . '

'Sorry to interrupt, Flynn,' said Rachel, tapping him on the shoulder and not sounding sorry at all. She threw a dismissive glance at Pru but then returned her whole focus to Flynn. 'But shouldn't we make our announcement soon?'

Pru recoiled from Flynn's embrace. She stepped backwards, tilting her head to give him a wide-eyed reproachful stare. He could almost feel her saying,

See, I told you so.

'In a moment, Rach,' he said. 'There's no rush.'

'No, I suppose there isn't.' Rachel's eyes locked with Pru's but she gave nothing away in her bland blue stare. She shrugged as though it was all the same to her. 'Don't be too long, though. I'd like to get the ball rolling.'

Flynn attempted to pull Pru back into his arms as Rachel gracefully moved away, dodging other dancers with her elegant, economic sway.

'You'd better go,' said Pru with blunt gruffness, resisting him and frowning in Rachel's direction.

'Trying to get rid of me, Amaryllis? Sorry, but no can do. We haven't finished our dance. Or our conversation. I'm just getting warmed up.' His hand rested boldly on her hip.

'Huh.' Pru hiked up his hand to her waist. 'You'd better cool down instead because Rachel's already on the stage. It's time to get your announcement over and done with.'

Flynn glanced over. Sure enough, Rachel had climbed up on the makeshift karaoke stage and was demanding attention by clapping her small, neat hands.

'Quiet everyone. Flynn and I have something important to tell you all . . .' she shouted over the rowdy partygoers.

So much for waiting, thought Flynn irritably. It was typical of Rachel to plough on ahead and not consider another person's wants when she had a goal of her own. He glanced down at Pru and said with rueful acceptance, 'I'll be back in a moment. This won't take long and then we can continue our discussion while we dance some more.'

'But Flynn . . .'

Her eyes were wide and hurt and Flynn couldn't understand why. He smiled gently, 'I told you, no buts. I'll be as quick as I can. Wait for me, sweetheart. Promise . . .'

'I'm promising nothing,' she declared, her lashes sweeping down to hide any further emotion in those puppy-soft eyes.

Flynn hesitated, wondering what was going on in that cute head of hers. He pulled her towards him in a brief hug and then let her go. 'I'll be back in no time, you'll see.'

He made his way to the stage and stepped up next to Rachel. As he slid his arm around Rachel's waist, his eyes sought out Pru. But where was she? He caught a flash of pink disappearing through the door. Dammit, she was leaving already!

He was tempted to chase after her, but there was the announcement to make and Rachel wouldn't take it lightly if he ducked out on her now. He'd have to get it over with quickly and then follow Pru outside and find out what was bugging her, because surely something was making her touchier than a cow separated from its calf. Something wasn't right and he sure intended to find out what and fix it.

It took a while for him to disengage himself from the congratulations that followed his and Rachel's announcement. Finally managing to escape, he went outside on to the verandah where he'd sat with Pru earlier in the day.

The street was cool, moonlit and silent. At first he couldn't locate Pru and presumed she'd taken herself off somewhere private. He was about to start searching the place inch by inch when he heard a small, watery sniff and he realised she was tucked deep in the dark shadows of the general store's building. Though he could only see her dimly, an aura of sadness clung to her slight, wraith-like frame as she leant in a defeated hunch against the wall. He yearned to gather her close and comfort her, even if he didn't understand what was upsetting her.

'Amaryllis?' he called softly.

'I heard the cheering,' she answered in a tight, strained voice edged with tears. 'Congratulations, Maguire.'

'Thanks.' He stood in front of her and stared down into her shadowed face, unsuccessfully trying to read her expression.

'When's the big day?' she asked after a minute's awkward silence.

'The contracts will be signed within the next week.'

'Contracts? That's sounds rather dried and business-like. But then I suppose that's how it's done up here in the North-West.' She didn't sound too thrilled. In fact she'd sounded as bugged as an angry wasp caught in a cobweb.

'Well, yes.' He ran his hand through his hair, scratching the back of his head, perplexed as to why she was so mad. 'But I don't think we're any different from anywhere else. It's sound business to get the deal sewn up good and tight at the earliest opportunity. That's all we're doing.'

She snorted, her derision obvious. She was making out the deal was something sordid.

'So there's no room for sentiment,' she said flatly.

'Business is business, Amaryllis. If you throw sentiment in, then it can get a little sticky. Surely you understand that?' Where the hell was this leading, he wondered.

'So you don't love her?' she shot back with blunt force, surprising him.

Flynn felt the full blast of her accusing gaze through the darkness. She was upset and angry, but why? 'Who don't I love?' he asked carefully.

'Rachel.'

He frowned. 'Sure I do. I'm extremely fond of her, but what's that got to do with anything?'

'I would have thought a lot, otherwise what's the point in getting married.' Again she sounded buzzed off.

'Married?' Flynn exclaimed. 'Who said anything about getting hitched?' He stared at her in bewilderment, wishing he could read her expression, cursing the shadows for masking her face.

'You and Rachel did.'

'We did?'

'Your important announcement,' she snapped.

Enlightenment flooded his brain. 'You thought we were getting married? That Rachel and I were announcing our engagement tonight?' He slapped his jean-clad thigh and threw back his head, laughing with cathartic amusement. 'Good one, Amaryllis. Is that why you're so snitchy? Are you jealous, my sweet?' He ruffled her hair, relieved.

'I take it from your reaction, I've got it wrong?' Her voice was wary but still sharp, as if she didn't quite know what was going on.

'Completely. I'm not getting jinkered to anyone. I saw what it did to my dad. Nope, I'm not jeopardising the station again for any woman. No, ma'am.' He slapped his thigh again as if to underline his point.

'So what was the announcement about?' she asked, with more than a little curiosity lacing her words.

'Rachel and I have scored a contract to supply organic beef to Indonesia. It'll mean a big boom in these parts. More work, more money. It'll benefit everyone. Even your dad.'

'Oh, well, congratulations then,' said Pru again, this time sounding much happier.

'And this time you mean it.'

'I did before!' she said indignantly.

'Didn't sound like it!'

'Well, I did.' She pouted and they both knew she was lying.

'Does this mean that you'll come back in and finish our dance?'

'I might.' She shrugged her shoulders, not wanting to make it too easy for him, he suspected.

He chuckled. 'Or better still, we could carry on here.' He reached down and took her hand, hauling her to her feet. She staggered slightly in her high-heeled sandals and Flynn took advantage of her misbalance to fold her into his arms.

'Now this is much better,' he said. 'Just you and me and the moonlight.' They swayed slowly to the muffled bass beat of the bar room music, Flynn holding her close and snug against his body.

As she sighed and relaxed against him, Flynn's lips skimmed her hair, and his fingers made a slow inventory of her spine. He felt her shiver deliciously beneath his caress. Her own responding touch was tentative and shy but no less sweet as her fingertips brushed along his jaw and fleetingly whispered across his lips. Time stood still for a priceless moment, suspended and unimportant against their exquisite, unfurling passion. Flynn gently caught one of her fingers between his teeth, causing a deep, ragged sigh to escape from Pru as his tongue moistly caressed the tip.

'Sweetheart,' he said, his mouth releasing her finger as he responded to her sigh. He lowered his head to kiss her.

Pru quivered as his mouth sought hers.

'Flynn . . . ' she whispered in awe.

'Flynn? Flynn? Are you there?'

Rachel's louder, more strident voice sliced through the darkness, over-riding Pru's gentle murmuring of his name.

Rachel!

Flynn muttered a curse under his breath. What was with the woman! Her timing was atrocious. 'Over here, Rach,' he said, not letting go of Pru, instead holding her tighter just in case she decided to slip away from him into the shadows.

'Oh,' said Rachel when she saw them standing entwined together. 'I do hope I'm not interrupting.'

'No, you're not interrupting any-thing,' said Pru with hasty politeness as she tried to escape from Flynn's arms, just as he suspected she would.

'Yes, you are,' said Flynn, holding Pru even more firmly. 'What do you want, Rachel?'

'You're needed inside. Lew's on the phone. Seems your new bull has busted the fence and is off romancing the girls.'

Flynn cursed again but this time for different reasons. 'Damn bull. He's as cranky as they come.'

He inwardly warred with his conscience. He so wanted to stay and carry on kissing Pru with a thoroughness bordering on madness. But he needed to deal with the darn bull. Duty, as always, had him in its vice-like grip. The station always won out.

'I'm sorry, Amaryllis,' he said with a regretful shake of his head. 'But I'll have to go before he does any major damage.' He gave her a quick squeeze around the waist and dropped a kiss on her nose. 'I'll be in touch as soon as I can.' And then he was gone, sucked into the warm velvet darkness of the night.

Pru watched him leave, all too aware Rachel was staring directly at her. The melting heat engulfing her a moment ago was cooling fast under the other woman's frost.

'I'd best get back behind the bar,' Pru said and took a couple of steps towards the door.

'Not so fast, Ms Stark.' Rachel held out a cool, firm hand to halt her progress. 'I want to talk to you about Flynn.'

'Can't it wait? I should really be helping Dad. I've already been gone longer than I intended.'

'No, I don't think it can wait.' Rachel dropped her hand once she sensed Pru would hear her out.

'Go on, then.' Pru wrapped her arms around her torso, protecting herself against the chilly night air as well as against whatever this frigidly controlled woman was going to say. Instinctively, she knew she wasn't going to like it.

'Flynn's a decent man. One of the best you'll ever meet,' said Rachel abruptly.

Okay, so the woman wanted to share a character profile on Flynn. Was that it?

'And?'

'He's special.'

'Yes, from the little I know of him, I'd say he was,' she agreed tentatively. It was impossible to read Rachel's face, but Pru had the impression Rachel was smiling. It didn't make her feel good. She was sure it wasn't a cosy sort of smile between friends. More of a cobra's smug smirk with a mouse just before it ate it.

'I hear you met him in Bali,' Rachel stated.

'Yes.'

'Not such old friends then.'

'No,' admitted Pru and wished she could have said otherwise.

'As I said, he's a decent man and I would hate to see him taken in by a woman like you.'

'And what's that supposed to mean?' Pru's hackles rose immediately. She'd been right. Rachel was going in for the kill.

'You know exactly what I mean! Flynn reckons you're a nice girl, but from where I'm standing you're nothing but a cheap tart. Keep away from him, Ms Stark. Flynn isn't for the likes of you.'

'I'm as good as anyone else,' she said, stung.

'Not nearly. Flynn needs someone with class and breeding. Two things you lack. I, on the other hand, have both.'

'You sound like one of his pedigree cattle. I applaud you. Maybe you should enter the next agricultural show. I'm sure you'll win a red rosette.'

There was a sharp intake of breath. 'He'd be a fool to get caught up with a good-time girl like you.'

Prudence had the hysterical urge to laugh. Since when had Pru, a staid primary school teacher who'd bored her fiancé into dumping her, morphed into a good-time girl? But instead, she said, 'He doesn't think so.'

'Oh, he's just acting like that young bull of his. The scent of an available woman is tantalising him and tempting him to go where he shouldn't. You're new. Exciting. You really shouldn't set any store over what he says.'

Pru felt miffed. 'Let's get one thing straight, Ms Burnley. I'm a big girl now and if I want Flynn Maguire, I'll take Flynn Maguire, any which way I can, and I won't bother seeking your permission, that's for sure.'

'You're asking for trouble,' Rachel ground out, her controlled, clipped voice vibrating fury.

'No, you are by trying to tell me how to run my life. Butt out, Rachel. I'm not interested in your established family pettiness or genealogy lines. I have my own life to lead. But hey, perhaps it's time there was new blood in Ibis Springs. Too much interbreeding can cause problems, you know.'

Rachel gasped. 'How dare you.'

'I dare.'

'Flynn is mine.'

'No! Flynn is his own man and it's up to him who he sees and what he does. You don't own him, Rachel. Nobody does. Give the guy a break.'

In the moonlit street the two women glared at each other. The deadlock was broken by a slight scuffle from the depths of inky shadows. Pru spun around and tried to pierce the gloom but her night-time vision was zilch. It must have been a stray cat, or maybe a possum. She swung back to Rachel and said, 'I'm going back inside. Some of us have work to do.'

'You have to understand,' said Rachel, once again holding hard on to Pru's arm to prevent her from leaving, her voice low and throbbing. 'Flynn's dad got tied up with the wrong type of women and it almost cost them the station with payouts and legal fees. Flynn's worked hard to make it viable again. If you start messing him around, playing with his head, his heart, you could destroy everything he's worked for these past few years.'

Pru listened in silence. Flynn had said as much a few minutes before. Rachel wasn't lying. She really did care about Flynn's welfare, about the man and about his beloved cattle station. Pru wasn't sure if they came as a complete package in Rachel's eyes, but that wasn't the issue here.

'I understand him,' Rachel carried on. 'I'll support and work with him to make the station successful. I know the demands of station life, the grit and determination needed. I know how hard it can be. I'm the right person for the job. Not you with your soft city ways and inexperience.'

Pru sighed and said tetchily, 'I'm not seeking a life-time commitment from Flynn. I just want a bit of fun. So does he.' And he was the perfect antidote to get her over Dean. He'd already done a lot to appease her hurt and humiliation.

'But he's a man of integrity. What's fun to you may not be the same to him. He's already attracted to you. It won't take much to get him involved, whatever he says about not wanting to. He hasn't been in a steady relationship for a long time. He's ripe to fall, especially with you strutting around in those clothes. He won't stand a chance.'

'A woman has a right to wear what she likes,' said Pru defensively. Okay, so she still wasn't completely at home wearing clothes that were so scanty and tight they belonged in the doll's clothes section of a toyshop. She knew Rachel had a valid point and it didn't help her temper.

'A woman does, I agree, but with you dressed like that. Flynn can be reeled in at any time. I don't care if I hurt your feelings by being blunt because it's Flynn I want to protect.'

'You care for him.' It was a statement, not a question.

'Who wouldn't? He's a special man. But he doesn't look at me like he looks at you. I realise that and though it hurts, I'm prepared to have him anyway I can. But while I'm waiting for him, I don't want him getting hurt by the likes of you. I want you to leave before it's too late, before you spoil everything.'

Pru's anger suddenly dissipated. She wasn't here to mess up people's lives. She didn't want another heartbreak, or to cause one, because she knew how painful it could be. She should walk away from Ibis Springs and not look back.

'Okay.' She sighed again, both deep

and long. It was time to be boring and sensible again. 'I'll do my utmost to keep him at arm's length for the rest of my stay here.'

'I'd appreciate it.'

'Yeah, right.'

'And I think it would be best for you to leave at the earliest opportunity.'

'Best for whom, I wonder?'

'All of us.'

Well, Pru couldn't argue with that.

7

The next day dawned bright and sunny but it might as well have been sheeting down with freezing winter rain because Pru was depressed to her very core and was barely noticing her exotic Australian surroundings. The blues had descended on her like a thick, matted blanket of soggy cotton wool ever since her conversation with Rachel. In her heart she knew Rachel was right, that she should leave Ibis Springs and Flynn before anyone got hurt. But it didn't mean she had to like the idea.

Jimmy's Place was a mess after the party, but at least it kept Pru occupied. She checked with the bus company first thing, and then every hour from then on, but the strike was still in progress. There was no chance of an immediate escape, which was rotten luck because now she was on tenterhooks in case

140

Flynn came into town to find her. She had no intention of telling him she was leaving. She didn't want a confrontation. She was just going to run, the coward that she was, and get clean away.

But what if he did come? She had to admit that a secret part of her hoped he would. And, face it; it wouldn't be her fault but the bus strike's.

Of course, she'd definitely try her hardest to leave Ibis Springs before that actually happened, but if Flynn fronted up before the strike was over, he'd be a hard man to avoid. For goodness sake, he wasn't the sort of man she could just ignore. One little peek at him would cause an urge the size of a canyon to engulf her and make her want to fling herself at him, feel his arms around her, have his lips fuse to hers, feel his heart in rhythm next to hers.

Damn but it had been bad luck Rachel had interrupted them last night, before he'd actually kissed her. Now the throb of unrequited lust beat in her blood, a tattoo of need, yearning for release.

How on earth was she going to freeze Flynn out if he did come to Jimmy's?

Well, she wouldn't be able to, would she?

She was one lost cause!

Perhaps, to avoid temptation, she should hitch a lift out of Ibis Springs on the next available truck, run away, fast! Good plan. If only there was a convenient truck handy.

'You are one glum chick,' said Toni, Jimmy's cook, who'd been giving Pru a hand with the cleaning. She was several years older than Pru and almost six foot tall with tattoos and piercings over much of her body. She looked like a biker's moll with her jeans, leather vest and big hennaed hair. Pru had discovered from the moment she'd first met Toni that, for all her startling appearance, the woman had a heart of purest gold.

But it didn't mean Pru was going to tell her of her Flynn-inspired misery.

'Must be post-party blues,' she said with a dismissive shrug and carried on drying and stowing the mountain of beer glasses.

'I didn't think you were enjoying the party that much to suffer a downer once it was over. I reckon all the spunk went out of you after the big boss man left last night,' said the other woman shrewdly, waggling her thinly plucked and kohl-pencilled eyebrows to make sure her point wasn't missed.

'Ah.' Pru inwardly groaned. Had she been that transparent? She prayed no one else but Toni had noticed.

'And you're bugging the bus company like you want out of here pretty quick,' carried on Toni.

'I do. So what? It's time I moved on.'

'Who are you kidding?'

'Not you, obviously.'

'Wanna talk about it, babe?'

'No. There's nothing to talk about.'

'That's cool.' Toni stacked clean glasses on to a shelf behind the bar for a while and hummed a country and western song about lost love under her breath. 'Why don't you do something to perk yourself up?' she then said.

Pru sighed. Obviously Toni wasn't going to let the matter drop. 'Such as?'

'Give yourself a new hair colour. I always find it works as a pick-me-up.'

'I don't have any hair dye,' she said flatly.

'Be creative, babe. Use food colouring. Jimmy's got a few bottles in the back storeroom.'

'Food colouring?' Who'd have thought? Certainly not Pru.

'Works for me,' Toni said nonchalantly.

Pru grinned, suddenly entranced by the notion. After all, hadn't she told her sister Kat that hair dyeing was on her wish list for new adventurous past times? And it was far better to focus on changing her hair colour than mooning over Flynn. 'What a good idea,' she said and they both threw down their tea towels and scuttled towards the storeroom.

'Cochineal pink, snazzy green or electric blue. What's it to be?' asked Toni as they inspected the store's shelves a few moments later.

Pru couldn't decide. In reality, she couldn't picture herself sporting any of those colours with confidence. But Toni was on a roll and wasn't going to be put off by Pru suddenly turning wimpy on her. Toni placed the bottles into a bag and made Pru do a lucky dip.

Pru pulled out a bottle and pulled a face. Perhaps this wasn't such a good idea . . .

'Cochineal it is, babe,' said Toni briskly. 'Let's do it before the place gets busy. And before you chicken out!'

★　★　★

Flynn's utility truck skidded to a halt outside of Jimmy's. Flynn unfolded himself from the dusty vehicle and slammed the door. He'd been caught up with vital station work for two whole days and all the while he'd been chafing at the bit to get into town and get his fix of Pru. Their interrupted kiss was haunting him, giving him heartburn. His gut clenched every time he remembered lowering his mouth towards her lush lips. Oh, how he'd wanted to taste them! He still did, dammit, and was eaten up with a consuming need that churned in his belly and made sleep impossible.

But he'd have to be patient. Even now there wouldn't be the time to finish what they'd started. He only had a few hours before he was due to leave Ibis Springs to meet with some delegates in Perth regarding the organic beef business. He really shouldn't be here. He couldn't afford the time to see Pru, but the woman was addictive. He missed her. He wanted her. He ached for her . . .

The ache banished as soon as he saw her.

Replaced by sharp shock.

'Good grief!' His voice just about failed him.

The vibrant pink hair was something else. It matched her scrap of skirt and lipstick but that was the only thing going for it. It clashed with everything else in the immediate vicinity.

'Your hair!' he bellowed as incredulity morphed to outrage.

Pru spun around and gave him a wide grin. 'Haven't we had this conversation before?'

'But, Amaryllis!'

'Don't you like it?' She challenged.

'Like isn't a word I would even think to use. What have you done?' His voice rose further.

'I thought it was a cheerful change.'

'I prefer brown. Even blonde was a little too much for my taste.'

'Both too boring, Flynn.'

'Sweetheart, you're exciting enough without going pink on me, believe me.' He shook his head, exasperated.

Pru did a twirl. 'That's a very sweet thing to say, Mr Maguire.'

Flynn's body clenched. She was so damned sassy and sexy, even with her crazy pink hair. He wanted her then and there.

Instinctively, he reached for Pru but she carried on twirling out of his grasp until she hit the bar. She slipped behind it and grinned from her safe vantage point.

'What can I get you, Mr Maguire? Coffee? Beer? Juice?'

You, he felt like saying.

But, darn it, he had to be sensible. This was the monotonous story of his life: duty before pleasure, every damn time.

He tipped back his wide-brimmed bush hat and then rammed his hands deep into his pockets to prevent himself from reaching for her. If he touched her, he'd get side-tracked and miss his business appointment, which couldn't happen. Too many people depended on him to bring off this deal successfully.

'I've come to say goodbye,' he said instead after a couple of deep, steadying breaths. 'I've got to go away on business for a few days.'

'Oh.' Her smile slipped and some of the sparkle went out of her eyes, or was that just his wishful thinking?

'I wish I didn't have to go but it's urgent. It's to do with this new meat export business.'

'Oh,' she said again and bit down on her lower lip, dropping her gaze to stare at the counter. She scratched at a mark on the formica with her finger, supposedly absorbed in the small task.

'But I wanted to make sure you'd still be here when I got back.' She was silent. 'Will you be?' he probed.

Her finger froze mid-action. Her shoulders stiffened. But she didn't raise her head. And she sure didn't answer him.

Suddenly he couldn't resist any longer. He had to touch her. He leaned over the bar and tentatively wrapped a psychedelic pink strand of hair around one of his fingers. He stared musingly at the brightly coloured hank and tugged it gently, asking her to raise her head. His eyes locked with hers. Pru's widened and dilated so they were dark pools, desirable and deep enough for a man — this man — to drown in. Flynn couldn't think of a better way to meet his fate. He began to tip his face towards her, inhaling her sweet honeysuckle scent as he drew nearer.

She gasped and pulled away a split second before their lips met.

'What are you doing?' she said with a breathlessness that sounded as if she'd just sprinted a couple of hundred metres in double-quick time.

'Trying to kiss you,' he replied, his voice reverberating with his own telltale huskiness.

'Well, don't, Flynn,' she whispered. 'Anyone could just march in here and see us.'

'Is that a problem?'

'Yes.'

'Why?'

'Because . . . because . . . it is.'

'But, honey, it's so right.' He smiled and reached for her again.

Pru jumped back and held her hands

up defensively. 'No way. I'm out of here as soon as those Greyhound buses are running again. Believe me, Maguire.'

Flynn jerked himself upright and rammed his hands back into his jeans' pockets, the force almost ripping holes in the material. He experienced a surge of frustration. Why must she leave? What was the point? He was certain she was as attracted to him as he was to her.

'Aw, come on,' he said, 'you don't really want to leave. What about us?'

'There is no us, Maguire.'

'What about the one-night stand replay we were going to have?'

Prudence fanned her hand in front of her face as if she was feeling far too hot for comfort. 'It's not going to happen. Probably never was.'

'And the other night meant exactly what? I can remember how you felt in my arms, Prudence. You were melting.'

She fanned faster. 'Okay, so we got a little carried away. But we were just fooling ourselves.'

'Really?'

'Yup.'

'Liar.'

'Not at all.'

'Okay, so tell me what happened to 'If I want Flynn Maguire, I'll take Flynn Maguire'? I'm very happy to be taken, let me tell you.'

'Oh my goodness!' she squeaked, her cheeks matching her hair. 'It was you out in the street, not a cat. Well, you shouldn't have been eavesdropping, Maguire. That's very rude.'

Flynn sighed in exasperation. It was the second time Pru had mistaken him for a cat.

'I came back because I wanted to kiss you goodbye, this time without Rachel as an audience. I wasn't eavesdropping on purpose, but you two seemed to have a great deal you wanted to say to each other. I couldn't hang around indefinitely waiting for you to finish up, not with that bull on the loose, so I split without seeing you.'

'Did you catch him okay?'

'Yes.'

'Had he done any damage?'

'No.'

'Is he secure now?'

'Yes. Stop changing the subject. So are you going to take me, Ms Stark?'

'No!' She blushed rosily. 'I've changed my mind.'

'Shame.' His jaw flexed. 'Why?'

'Just because.' Her eyes were wild and panic stricken and her blush deepened.

Flynn cocked his head to one side as an amazing thought occurred to him. But no. She was too confident. Too sassy . . . Too damn sexy. But nevertheless . . .

'Hey, babe, you're acting like a virgin.'

Whoosh. Her blush actually intensified. Her face grew pinker than her hair, which was saying something, and her mouth opened and shut rapidly without issuing a sound.

Flynn regarded her indulgently. That would explain a lot.

Pru was still doing her cochineal-carp routine.

'It's nothing to be embarrassed about, sweetheart,' he said gently.

'It's not the reason!' she managed to squeeze out through a throat that sounded full of sand. 'And who's embarrassed?' But her face had betrayed her. If anything, her cheeks had grown even pinker and Flynn couldn't hold back a chuckle.

'Then why so pink, Amaryllis? You'll have to change your hair colour if you're going to keep blushing so easily.'

'I only blush when people say stupid things!'

'Asking if you're a virgin isn't stupid.'

'Yes it is, considering our night together in Bali.' Her blush deepened to crimson and she refused to catch his eye.

For a couple of steady heartbeats, Flynn stared at her squirming body and fluttering, nervous hands. She rearranged some beer middies on the counter, brutally clinking the glasses with her agitated movements.

'Careful, you'll break them,' he said, stopping her hands with his. 'And actually, Amaryllis, nothing happened between us in Bali. You passed out cold after that fancy cocktail you insisted on drinking and I'm not the sort of man to take advantage in a situation like that.'

'But you said . . . You implied . . . ' She gasped, wrenching her hands away from his hold and covering her shocked eyes with her palms. Her lips thinned and a pulse hammered at the base of her throat. She was spitting mad. And mortified!

'I was teasing you. I thought you realised that.'

'No. No I didn't!' She was good and miffed and spoiling for a fight and he wasn't sure if it was because they hadn't done anything in Bali, or because he hadn't told her they hadn't.

'And I wouldn't have teased you if I'd realised. I would have come clean right from the start, promise.'

'Oh for goodness sake, it doesn't matter! I'm all grown up. I can take

155

teasing with the best of them.' She dashed her hand across her over-bright eyes again, nullifying the statement.

Flynn pursed his lips, deciding he had to know for certain. 'So you are still a virgin?'

'As if I'm going to tell you, Maguire!'

He continued to look at her expectantly, waiting for her answer.

'Oh, for heaven's sakes, go away! I've got nothing more to say to you.' She slammed her fist on the counter and glared at him. 'And especially not about . . . about my sex life.' Her chin lifted aggressively, challenging him to respond.

And he wanted to, but instead he glanced at his watch. He'd run out of time. He had to go, but hell, he'd much prefer to stay and sort things out with Prudence. He didn't want to leave her like this, so buzzing mad. Flynn itched to smooth out those angry furrows dimpling her brow and kiss her back into her usual buoyant good humour. 'It's a shame we can't discuss this now,

Amaryllis,' he said with regret.

'There's absolutely nothing to discuss,' she announced baldly.

'On the contrary, sweetheart, there's a whole heap of things we need to talk about. So please, no hopping on a bus before I get back. Let's give things a chance between us.'

'But . . . '

He went to touch her cheek but Pru recoiled. Flynn dropped his hand to his side.

'Don't worry,' he said with a wry smile. 'I'm not going to kiss you, at least not this time. But you just wait until I return because then there'll be no going back . . . ' He strode out from the bar, the flywire door slamming hard behind him.

To Pru, it was a depressingly final farewell because she didn't intend to be in cooee of Ibis Springs by the time Flynn returned. Whatever he said about giving their relationship a chance, she knew it was doomed because of her promise to Rachel,

And because she knew she wasn't the right sort of woman for him.

And because she knew she was on the rebound and too vulnerable to be thinking straight.

And because she was too boring and he was too special . . .

'Well that went well, I don't think,' said Toni from the open kitchen door, steam issuing behind her from the deep-fat fryer. 'Dang, if he isn't one hot man.'

'Too hot for me,' said Pru, flapping her hand again and hoping Toni wouldn't see the treacherous pooling of tears because, in spite of all those reasons she still wanted him like crazy.

'Nonsense. He's after you, babe. You're one lucky chick.'

'But I'm not after him.'

'Liar.'

'It's true. And even if I was, Rachel would have my guts for garters if I tried to hit on him.'

'Rachel Burnley doesn't own him, however hard she's been trying. And you know the old saying, all's fair in love and lust . . . '

Pru gave a watery chuckle.

'Yes, but I promised her I wouldn't get involved with Flynn.'

'Well, then there's that other over-used, but apt, saying, promises are made to be broken.'

'I'm not that sort of girl. I like to keep my promises.'

'No other woman would, given the grand prize. Come on Pru, isn't he worth fighting for?'

'I suppose.'

'Too right he is. Go for it, kid.'

'Perhaps.'

'I would and you'd be mad not to. He's already after you good and proper. And Rachel has had all the time in the world to fix her interests with him and it hasn't happened yet. So I reckon the coast is clear.'

'True.' Pru suddenly grinned, liking Toni's logic. 'You're right. He is worth it. He won't know what's hit him when he gets back from Perth.'

'That's what I like to hear, girl! Flynn Maguire, watch out because our Pru here is hot to trot.' Toni then turned her speculative gaze on Pru. 'Is it true, though? That you're still a virgin?' she said with a quizzical rise of her kohled brows.

Pru dropped her head in her hands. 'Why don't I just put an announcement up on Jimmy's notice-board!'

'Cool.'

'I was joking.'

'Oh. Never mind, then.'

'But it is a factor,' she confessed. 'I'm totally inexperienced in the seduction stakes.' Pru raised her head again, looking glum.

'So you do need cheering up!' Toni sounded much too happy about that.

Uh-oh. Pru wasn't ready for another of Toni's cheering up sessions. She hadn't recovered from the first one yet. 'No, I'm fine, really,' she said with a rush of panic.

'No, I feel you need a tonic, a confidence booster.'

'I think I'll stick to the pink hair a little while longer, Toni, but thanks all the same,' said Pru hastily, knowing full well where this was leading. She hadn't admitted it to Flynn, but even she found the pink experience an unnerving one.

'I was going to suggest a couple of extra earrings. Or maybe even a tattoo,' said Toni serenely. 'I always find a little piercing good for the soul.'

'I think I'm worried about your soul,' said Pru with a great deal of feeling.

'Not chicken, babe?'

The soft challenge brought Pru up short. She was meant to be re-inventing herself. Being adventurous. And what were a few stud holes and a tattoo in the scheme of things?

'Okay, maybe a small tattoo?' Pru conceded with false bravado. 'But I don't want it to be too obvious.'

'As in?'

'Where people can see it. I don't want to look as if I've joined the navy.'

'So you are chicken. You're worried

what people will say.' Toni rolled her eyes in disgust.

'Not me. I'm just concerned that I may not like it. Or it may clash with my outfits.'

'Baloney. Okay, so I'll do one on your butt. Is that hidden enough for you?'

'But that's rather personal . . . '

'Darlin', I'm beyond being shocked by anything.'

Pru believed her. But was she beyond the shocking stakes?

'Let me tell you some of the places I've put tattoos for people.'

'No, I'd rather you didn't. Too much information,' said Pru quickly, holding up her finger to stop her. She didn't trust the wicked gleam in Toni's eyes. 'My backside will do just fine.'

'So what d'ya want?' Toni asked her. 'Any requests?'

'No. I can't think of anything specific off the top of my head. Just do a little pretty one of maybe a flower or something and make it very, very small and unobtrusive.'

'You are so bourgeois.'

That stung. Remember how she was going to leave all her boring old character traits behind? Live dangerously for once? 'Do your damnedest, then,' she said rashly.

'Okay, just leave the design and details to me, babe. This is going to be fun.'

But Pru didn't find it fun at all. In fact, Pru didn't want to dwell on the experience of that afternoon. In hindsight, she wondered what, apart from bravado, had possessed her to have a tattoo. She'd hated needles since she was a kid having her immunisation jabs. She didn't even like sewing because she invariably pricked herself. And taking out splinters was a nightmare. The only consolation was she couldn't see the tattoo being done, because then she'd probably have passed out cold. As it was, the pain of having it drawn with a razor blade almost blacked her into unconsciousness. At least the blocking in of colour hadn't hurt so much.

And now she was the proud owner of a sore backside adorned with zinc and castor oil baby bottom cream and clear plastic food wrap. Toni had told her she had to do that to keep the tattoo moist to avoid scabbing. But what else was on her butt? Toni hadn't told her what she'd tattooed. She'd said it would be a nice surprise, but Pru wasn't so sure.

At the first opportunity, she went into Jimmy's small bathroom, which was the only room in the house with a mirror, to find out. Unfortunately the mottled mirror was above the sink and screwed into the wall. The only way Pru could view her derriere was to get a chair and stand on it, butt naked. She squinted in the mirror.

The tattoo was small and neat. Good.

It was colourful, which was also good.

It was a little red heart. Nice, she liked hearts.

With blue writing on it.

Hmm. Had writing been in the

equation? It appeared to be a name. She had to shuffle the chair closer to make out what was written.

Reading mirror writing wasn't one of Pru's special skills but even she could easily work out the one word Toni had flourishingly tattooed in blue ink: FLYNN.

'I'll kill her,' Pru muttered, jumping down from the wobbly chair and slapping back on her food wrap and clothes.

'I'll kill her,' she seethed as she stomped through the place hunting for Toni.

'I'll kill her,' she said as she winced when she whacked her bottom against the side of a bar table.

She finally bailed her up in the kitchen where Toni was cooking fish and chips for a customer.

'You witch!' hissed Pru, low so that Jimmy or the customer in the bar wouldn't hear her. 'Why did you tattoo Flynn's name on my butt?'

Toni laughed. 'Because, babe you're

as hot for him as he is for you.'

'Hot doesn't come into it. You have to change it, scrub it out. Do something!' The last word came out as a pathetic wail.

'Can't. That's it for life. Unless, of course, you get plastic surgery done. Or you could have laser treatment but it's very costly.'

'Omigod.' Pru felt faint with shock. She was stuck with Flynn's name inked on her backside.

'Don't worry, Pru. True love will win out.'

'Is that another one of your rotten sayings, Toni, because if it is it sucks!'

'Look, babe, in all the time I've known Flynn I've never seen that look in his eyes he has when he looks at you. It's cute. Not to say sexy.'

Pru felt a rush of heat that had nothing to do with the deep fryer and hot weather. Then she regarded the blandly smiling Toni with suspicion.

'And just how long have you known Flynn Maguire, Toni?'

'Four or five months max,' Toni said promptly.

'Omigod.' Now Pru had gone cold through and through. Toni was a nutter. Pru should never have trusted her to do the tattoo, just as she shouldn't have trusted her with her hair colour.

'Flynn must never, ever see that tattoo,' she declared, vowing to ring the bus company yet again so she wouldn't miss the bus when it finally came through. What would Flynn say if he found out about it? Or saw it? And with Toni and her loose mouth there was a good chance that most of Ibis Springs would find out about it by the end of the day! She shuddered to think of the fall out. Flynn would probably throttle her. Or fall about laughing. Both scenarios were equally bad.

No way was she going to hang around to find out, even if it meant thumbing a lift or hiking out of town.

'Well, if Flynn does discover the tatt,' said Toni with reasonable logic, 'then we know you're making progress in the loving stakes because you'll both be butt naked. And once he sees that sweet tattoo he won't doubt your feelings for him at all. He'll be thrilled. So many people get caught up in knots about declaring their love, but you won't have that problem. Just flutter your eyelashes, drop your daks and moon him, babe, and he'll be yours.'

'Am I meant to be grateful?' said Pru incredulously, whilst madly trying to blot out the image of her and Flynn together and naked.

An affair with Flynn Maguire would be much too much for her to handle, she decided. He was too special for her. Dean had been right. She was boring.

'You'll thank me down the track,' said Toni with a dirty, throaty laugh. She winked at Pru as she bit into a sizzling hot chip and then took the plate of food out to the customer waiting in the bar.

Pru rubbed her throbbing temples, trying to relieve the tension headache swiftly taking hold. It was clamping her head in an iron vice. She felt totally out of her depth.

She had to leave as soon as possible, because there was no telling what could happen between her and Flynn the next time they met.

8

'Want to come riding, Pru?' asked Lew. He was leaning against the bar and downing an ice-cold beer at Jimmy's.

It was early evening. The bus strike was still grinding on, Flynn was still away and Pru was still as antsy as an expectant cat overdue for her litter of kittens. The idea of getting away from Jimmy's Place for a few hours and doing something different was extremely appealing. But there was one snag.

'I'd love to, but I can't ride,' said Pru and pulled a face.

'No problem. We've got an old mare that's the sweetest thing ever born. Anyone can ride her. She's just about bombproof.'

'You're not just saying that to lull me into a false sense of security?'

'As if.' He grinned. 'It'll be like riding on air.'

'Now I know you're lying!'

'Trust me.'

'Okay. I will. Riding the range sounds perfect after a day stuck behind the bar.' Pru was already picturing herself out on the sun-baked plains like a character in an ancient John Wayne movie.

'Can you be ready in ten minutes?'

'You bet. Er . . . Flynn won't be there, will he?'

She hated herself for asking but she had to know. Just because he hadn't been into Jimmy's didn't mean Flynn hadn't returned to his precious Ibis Springs Station and was there catching up on chores. She'd learnt from Toni all about his well-developed sense of duty and how it took precedence over pleasure. There was no guarantee he wasn't already well ensconced at home. No way did she want to bump into him in a hurry, not after their last embarrassing conversation, which was burning a hole in her brain as the scene replayed over and over again with mortifying monotony.

And then there was the little issue of the tattoo. Similarly that was burning a right royal hole of its own, right through the material of her stretchy mini skirt. Or at least that was how it felt to Pru. Since having the wretched tattoo done, she was awfully self-conscious about it and felt, inexplicably, that everyone could see it even though it was well hidden under her clothes.

'Nah, he's still off with the hot-shot city lawyers or doing whatever he's doing with Rachel.' Lew cracked his knuckles and drained his beer in a single gulp.

Pru did a double take at his fed-up tone, registering his slumped shoulders and dejected droop to his eyelids. Something didn't equate here and she didn't think it was because Flynn was dealing with the legal profession. So that just left Rachel and as far as she'd gathered since being in town, there wasn't much love lost between Lew and the ice woman.

But perhaps it was just a smokescreen for something completely opposite?

'So I take it you don't like Flynn and Rachel being together?' she hazarded later as she and Lew drove out to the station in Flynn's utility truck, the red dust flying behind them like a proud red flag.

Lew slanted her a glimmer of a smile. 'Is it that obvious?'

'Not really.' But she recognised unrequited love when she saw it, because she was suffering from it too, thanks to Flynn. 'You like Rachel?'

'Can't help myself. I don't like what she is or what she stands for, but the woman really gets to me. Has done for years.'

'So why don't you do something about it?'

'Because she's made it plain it's Flynn and the station she wants, not some dirt-poor farmhand with a non-pedigree background.'

'Cattle barons — or would that be baronesses? — and their breeding lines,

don't you just love them,' she sighed.
'But don't belittle yourself, Lew. You're
an important part of Ibis Springs.
Without you, Flynn's station and
business wouldn't be as successful as it
is. He'd still be struggling to survive.
Even I've realised that in the short span
I've been here. You're just as much a big
man around here as Flynn Maguire.'

'Thanks for the vote of confidence.'
He sounded amused but not convinced.

'It's true,' she defended. 'Ask
anyone.' She started listing suitable
candidates.

'Okay, okay, stop! I believe you.
Thanks.'

'You're welcome.'

'But it doesn't mean a hill of beans to
Ms Burnley. I wasn't born with the
right connections.'

'That is such an outmoded idea!' she
said, outraged. 'Anyone with grit,
determination and flair can get on
nowadays. It's not what you are but
who you are that matters.'

'Breeding still counts for something

in the North-West.'

'Good grief, now you're sounding exactly like Rachel. She was spinning me the same line a few nights ago. I reckon you two are made for each other! You can both discuss pedigrees over your cornflake bowls.' She gave him a friendly punch on the arm.

Lew smiled but shook his head. 'No, we're not compatible. I don't rate in her scheme of things.'

'Then make yourself rate. Get her interested in you and nobody else. Show her what you're made of. Fight for her.' Now she was sounding like Toni. If Pru wasn't careful, the next thing she'd be doing would be offering to dye his hair orange and tattoo 'I love Rachel' across his nether regions.

Lew shook his head again. 'It's not that easy.'

'How hard have you actually tried, Lew? Or have you been admiring her from afar all these years? Goodness, you men can be slow when it comes to loving.'

'What is this? A relationship pep talk?'

'Yes! I think you should go for it. Grasp your dreams before it's too late.'

'And that's your motto for life?'

'Only in the past few weeks,' she admitted with a rueful sigh, thinking of how much time she'd wasted on her empty dreams with Dean, how monochrome her life had been until he'd dumped her and everything had swung into sharp, colourful focus. 'But let me tell you, in those weeks I've felt more alive than I ever thought possible. Not always happy, I must admit, but definitely alive.'

'I'll give it some consideration.'

'You should, because I don't think Rachel and Flynn actually love each other, you know, passionately. They're just used to being around each other. A habit, I guess. They're very fond of each other, but I don't think they're in love with each other.'

At least, she hoped they weren't! She was pretty sure they weren't because

Flynn wouldn't be showing her any interest. But perhaps it was only her wishful thinking . . .

Lew drove on without speaking for a few miles, avoiding the worst of the potholes pitting the red gravel road.

Finally he broke the silence. 'Since you've been here, Flynn's changed,' he said musingly. 'He's spending more time in town and seems preoccupied with things other than the station. He's been a lot less work-driven. And you seem to spark with him. So tell me, Pru, are you going to grasp that particular dream?'

'He's not on my dream agenda,' Pru said firmly. 'And we're talking about you and Rachel, not Flynn and me.'

'Cool it, kid. I don't want to interfere. Though it seems to me we could help each other here.'

'How so?' Though she didn't know if she wanted it spelled out. Lew's face had scrunched into a cunning expression, like a fox eying up a henhouse.

'How about we make the two of them

jealous by hanging out together?' he threw at her.

Pru had been right. He was cooking up something distasteful. She snorted. 'Yeah, right.'

'I mean it. Let's do it.'

He sounded serious which made her squirm uncomfortably. 'Why?' she asked warily, not really wanting to know the answer in case it got her into deeper, more dangerous waters with Flynn.

'It'll force them to take stock of their feelings. You never know my luck, Rachel might decide she doesn't like seeing you and me together and ditch her plans to marry Flynn.'

'It'll never work.'

It was Lew's turn to give a snort. 'Oh come on. It might. And I reckon it's worth a shot. Fight for love, you said. So how about it, Pru? Are you game to put your money where your mouth is and wade into battle? Or are you all talk?'

Pru nibbled her lower lip and then sighed. 'But I don't want to make Flynn jealous. I don't want to change the status quo between us. It would only complicate things.'

Pru knew she was being a coward. She wanted out. Completely. She'd decided these past few days she wasn't ready for another relationship. She was still on the rebound from Dean, or more realistically, from being engaged and believing she was in love and loved. She didn't want Flynn-induced troubles or heartache, which meant, of course, avoiding Flynn, just like Rachel wanted her to. Thank goodness he was still on his business trip. But she wished the wretched bus strike was over so she could ride out of Ibis Springs before his return.

'But it might help me with Rachel,' Lew appealed. 'I'm trying to be pro-active here, on your particular advice may I add, so why won't you help me? Please?'

'Okay, perhaps I'll do it. But I'm warning you, I might not be around to help for very long. I'm off as soon as those Greyhound buses are running.'

'I understand that, but will you think about it anyway?'

'Maybe, but no promises.'

'You're a good kid, Pru.'

'I said no promises, Lew.'

But Lew just grinned and began whistling a jaunty tune, which made Prudence feel she'd been conned. Perhaps he had insider knowledge about the bus strike and knew she was grounded in Ibis Springs for a good long while yet.

Perhaps she should be strong and just tell him it was a no-go . . .

Prudence was still inwardly debating with herself when they finally arrived at Ibis Springs Station. It was the first time Pru had been to Flynn's home and she was suitably impressed.

The property was vast and awe-inspiring for someone used to the grey, overcrowded London suburbs where houses and shops jostled for space and streets were jam-packed with nose-to-tail traffic. The Ibis Springs' homestead itself was low and sprawling, flanked by wide, shady verandahs. Lew told her the house had been built by Flynn's great-grandfather. He'd quarried the deep red stone from the property a hundred and fifty years before. There were several trees shading the house and sturdy timbered cattle yards several metres away. It was all situated in an oasis of green and looked like a rich, lustrous emerald gemstone in the golden savannah grassland.

The one thing the station did lack, though, was a garden. There were sad remnants of one but, Pru supposed, what with the scarcity of water and the absence of a woman's touch, it wasn't surprising it had been neglected. The men, she thought wryly, just wouldn't have the time or inclination to tend red, white and yellow tea roses and pink, trumpeting hollyhocks.

Lew and Prudence didn't go into the house, but skirted around it to enter a large barn. It was cool and dark inside the corrugated iron building, a stark contrast from the warm evening air outside. Pru wrinkled her nose at the mixed rich aroma of horses, dung, hay and leather.

The horses were already corralled and it wasn't long before Pru was astride her mount and feeling decidedly uneasy.

Her first thought was the animal was much larger than the sleepy seaside donkeys she'd ridden as a child. Her next thought was that it was also stronger and leaner and faster than those same little grey donkeys with their thick, shaggy coats and sleepy demeanours.

Could she cope? She fervently hoped so.

But the pretty bay mare was as quiet as Lew had promised and Pru felt almost comfortable after a while except, of course, for the tender area sporting her new tattoo. She'd worn her only pair of jeans and another of Jimmy's old T-shirts for the ride. Lew had furnished her with a battered wide-brimmed hat that had been hanging up by the horse tack, and a pair of scuffed brown boots. He stuck the hat on her head and quirked a smile.

'You don't look half bad. We'll make a jillaroo out of you yet, young Prudence.'

She grinned but kept her teeth clenched from the effort of holding on. 'Don't hold your breath, cowboy, I've decided this is a one-off.'

'Don't bank on it. You'll love it.'

Pru wasn't convinced. 'We'll see,' was all she said.

She rode numerous circuits of the enclosed corral with Lew shouting instructions on how to sit, what to do with her legs and how to hold the reins. But it didn't matter how many times she rode around the enclosure, Pru remained tense. She wasn't a natural at this riding lark. Where were the brakes, for heavens' sake? And why wasn't there a seatbelt when you needed it most?

'Relax,' called Lew from where he was perched on the rails. 'You look as though you're sitting in a dentist's chair rather than in a saddle. Relax and enjoy.'

'Actually, I think I'd prefer a trip to the dentist rather than this,' admitted Pru with a nervous laugh. 'Facing fillings, root canal work and all. I do not feel safe on this thing!'

'She's as easy as an armchair.'

'Your armchairs might move, Lewis, but mine don't!' she responded tartly.

'So you don't feel up to riding the plains, cowgirl?'

His disappointment was loud and clear and made Pru feel like a wimpy spoilsport. She sighed. 'Okay, maybe a little ride,' she said with deep reluctance.

Lew didn't need another invitation and was on his horse, tightening the girths, before Pru could say 'High-ho Silver' and withdraw her offer.

They headed off into what looked like a reality poster for the Never-Never. She could see for miles. There was nothing to hinder the horizon from stretching into nowhere.

So, she mused anxiously, what if her horse bolted? Would it ever stop? Would she ever be found? Heck, probably not!

Pru valiantly tried to keep her negative thoughts to herself. Hadn't she read somewhere that horses could sense what you were thinking? Did this horse know she was petrified? Best to block it out, then. Just relax and enjoy, like Lew said. Pretend it was a big, warm armchair taking her for a ride and not a fully paid up member of the equine family with long legs, sharp teeth and hard hooves. That was the ticket. Everything would be fine.

But in spite of her self-instruction, Pru remained stiff and tense. Her neck and shoulders hurt from the strain of holding the unnatural posture. Her bottom was sore, both from the saddle's friction and her darn tattoo.

This was not fun and she didn't feel adventurous, just scared.

After a while Lew asked her if she'd be okay while he galloped the fidgets out of his bay gelding. Pru was relieved to see him go and even more relieved her mare showed no desire to follow. The tension of remaining upright in the saddle began to ease as her confidence grew and soon Pru slumped into the saddle and let the reins go slack.

They ambled along and Pru almost, *almost* began to enjoy the ride. Lew was off in the distance, a speck in a cloud of dust. The sun had long lost its burning sting as it sunk low on the horizon. Yes, this ride was becoming ever-so-slightly enjoyable.

The ambling gait of the horse and the warm evening lulled Pru into a daze. It took her a while to register the drone of a far off engine. She sat up straighter in the saddle and scanned the rolling, pale gold hills and liquid blue sky. Finally she spotted the cause of the noise: a light aircraft, and it appeared to be heading in their direction.

The mare registered the engine noise about the same time as Pru. She fidgeted and ducked her head. Pru cack-handedly tried to gather up the slackened reins, her heart bumping up to her mouth while her stomach dipped to her toes. Suddenly the mare snorted and sidestepped, almost unseating Pru. Pru gave a wild clutch at the pommel with one hand and buried her fingers deep in the wiry black mane with the other. She murmured a few soothing words to the horse. It didn't take any notice. Pru didn't blame her, she was jabbering gibberish anyway.

As the plane drew closer, the horse grew more skittish, dancing a jig to rival any Irishman. It took all Pru's strength to hold on.

The plane was almost overhead when the mare reared wildly and took off like an Exocet missile towards the station, her hooves kicking up great balls of dust. Pru clung on desperately as the animal lengthened its stride like a seasoned racehorse and streaked for home. Pru attempted to slow its pace by pulling on the reins but decided, after a couple of abortive attempts, it was safer to hold on to the saddle and mane. If she didn't, she'd be hitting the deck at a hundred miles per hour, which wasn't something she was in a hurry to experience.

Horse and woman raced for the stockyards. The mare didn't check her stride as the rails of the corral loomed. Pru shut her eyes and prayed.

They were airborne.

Or at least Pru was.

And then suddenly she wasn't anymore.

Because she'd hit the dirt.

And hard!

★　★　★

'If you've killed her, I'll damn well kill you!' snarled a voice above Pru's jolted, aching body.

Pru was sure it was Flynn's voice, but it was almost unrecognisably harsh and raised in jagged fury that did nothing for her pounding head. But then, she reasoned, the voice couldn't belong to

Flynn because he was miles away in Perth. And anyway, she was too winded to give it much thought, too busy battling for breath and clutching her tightening chest that felt it was going to implode through lack of air.

All the oxygen had been forced from her lungs by the fall's impact. She tried to suck in air but it was an impossible task. She felt on the verge of unconsciousness. Dimly she was aware of someone kneeling down beside her. Hands, firm but gentle, explored her face, her body, feeling her pulse.

'Relax, honey. Don't fight it,' commanded the Flynn clone.

At last the air whooshed back in her lungs. She sucked in huge, juddering, life-giving breaths and then flopped back in the dirt, spread-eagled like a rag doll.

She lay there until her breathing was less laboured. Finally, she summoned the courage to crank open an eye. And there was Flynn. Yep, it was definitely Flynn. Even in her distressed state she registered he was wearing a crisp white shirt and light cords. Ever the gentleman farmer. He looked and smelled so good. Not like the horse pooh that was piled a couple of inches away from her head. And she was so pleased to see him. Her mouth worked to tell him so, but no sound issued forth.

Flynn beat her to it. 'Thank God. When I first saw you there, I thought you were dead!' he cracked out before roughly grabbing her by the front of her T-shirt and hauling her against his chest. His arms banded around her so hard she thought she was in danger of losing her lung capacity all over again.

'I could kill you for pulling that stunt,' he said into her hair, his voice unsteady and gruff.

He sounded as though he meant it and her eyes filled with tears, with one sliding down her dusty cheek.

'You damn stupid woman.' Flynn sounded rattled as he wiped away the tear with the roughened pad of his thumb. 'What the hell do you think you were playing at?'

'If you're going to shout and swear at me, you can push off again,' she muttered, sniffing and snapping shut her eyes again. Perversely, she clutched hold of his shirt in case he did decide to go. She snuggled closer, enjoying the sensation of being held tight. And then she must have passed out because everything went woozy, then black and then nothing.

'Pru? Pru?' From far away she felt someone touch her forehead.

'She might be concussed,' she heard Lew say. He sounded worried. Pru frowned in the mists of her unconsciousness. Concussed? Maybe. Every bone in her body jolted and cracked? Dead cert. Still alive? Hopefully!

'More than likely.' It was Flynn. His voice was low and angry. 'Why the hell did you put her on Dolores?'

Dolores? Oh, yes. The almost bomb-proof horse. She'd have words with Lew as soon as she was able!

Pru could feel herself tuning in and

out of the distant conversation. It felt so good to be lying in Flynn's arms rather than balancing on the back of that wild, spooked horse that had no respect for novice riders.

'How was I to know you'd come back today?' countered Lew. 'If you'd bothered telling me what you and Rachel were up to, I wouldn't have had Pru anywhere near that plane-hating horse.'

'I wasn't aware you were my keeper.'

'I'm not, but it wouldn't hurt to know your movements every once in a while. You're always off with Rachel, leaving me to run the place.'

'That's what you're paid to do.'

'But some communication would be helpful.'

'Remind me to furnish you with an itinerary next time I go anywhere. Perhaps Rachel will too, if you ask her nicely.'

'That's not what I meant.'

'Perhaps you'd like to spell out exactly what you do mean?'

Uh-oh. Even through her fogged consciousness, Pru could hear the escalating anger. She sighed and forced open her eyes with an effort. The two men were glaring at each other like a couple of pit-bull terriers. She'd have to intervene even if she'd rather close her eyes and sleep for a week.

'You fellas going to argue all night or are you going to help me up?' she murmured, raising her head a little and then wishing she hadn't as the pain whipped through her. She grimaced and lay back against Flynn.

Flynn was immediately all concern. 'Do you think you've broken anything?' he demanded.

'Only my pride.'

'Can you wiggle your toes? Your fingers?'

'Ta-da,' she said, obligingly doing just that, but it was with an effort. Every part of her body felt bruised and battered.

Flynn cursed and slipped an arm under her legs. 'Hasn't knocked the stuffing out of that smart mouth of yours,' he said.

'It'll take more than that, Maguire.'

'I don't doubt it.'

'Put me down, Flynn. I can walk.'

'Shut up, Pru. You're in no fit state to argue.'

'But I'm heavy. You'll put your back out.'

'Quit griping. I've carried you before.'

'But . . . '

'Good grief, woman, I think I preferred you winded and out cold. At least you didn't talk rubbish.'

'Have it your own way.' She attempted to stick her nose in the air.

'I shall, believe me.'

But she didn't hear him. She'd drifted into blissful black nothingness again.

When she awoke the next time, there was a cold cloth plastered to her forehead and she was lying prone on a leather couch. The snap of her jeans had been undone and her borrowed riding boots had been discarded revealing her stripy yellow and pink socks. Both men were hovering over her, wearing identical worried expressions. Flynn had a smear of dirt across his cheek and his pristine clothes were now liberally coated with red dust, no doubt from kneeling on the ground in the corral and then carrying her to the house.

She tentatively pushed herself up on her elbows and gave a rueful grin-cum-wince. 'Hi, guys. Have I been out long?'

'No, thank goodness,' answered Flynn. 'But I'd best take you into the medical centre and get you checked over. You might have done yourself some real damage.'

'No,' Pru immediately recoiled from the suggestion. 'No doctors.' She didn't want the fuss, or to go anywhere near a hospital. She hated hospitals.

'It won't be a doctor. He only flies in once a week. It'll be our nurse. Joannie.'

'But I don't want to go. I feel fine.'

'You might have broken something,

or have concussion.'

'I'm okay.' She crossed her arms across her chest and glared at him. He crossed his arms and glared back. This wasn't getting them anywhere. Pru decided she'd better break the deadlock.

'So what happened to the safe-as-houses, bombproof horse?' she asked, turning her frustration on Lew.

'What can I say? Dolores hates planes,' said Lew looking suitably sheepish. 'But I thought she'd be okay. I wasn't expecting Flynn to fly in this evening.'

Pru gasped in surprise. 'You flew? It was you in that plane?' Pru stared at Flynn as if he'd actually sprouted a full set of wings and flown unaided.

'Of course I flew.' He was dismissive. 'You wouldn't expect me to drive to Perth, would you? It'd take far too long.'

'I suppose I hadn't really thought about it.' Pru pondered about the logistics and then said accusingly, 'So you could have taken me with you? Left me in Perth so I could resume my travelling rather than waiting in Ibis Springs for the bus strike to finish?'

'I suppose I could have. Remind me to take you next time.' His tone was as dry as two-week-old stale bread. 'But for now, I think I'd better take you back to Jimmy's. At least you'll be close to Joannie if you develop any problems.'

'Don't worry about it, boss. I'll take Prudence home,' cut in Lew. 'After all, she is my date.'

'What?' Flynn's eyes became slits as he stared at them both with cold scrutiny. 'You were on a date?'

Pru mentally cringed. So Lew was going ahead with his suggestion to make Flynn and Rachel jealous. But was this really the best time to start? She warily glanced at Flynn. He didn't look happy. There wasn't a vestige of his usual warm good humour. In fact he looked downright flinty.

'It wasn't a date as such,' she rushed in to say, feeling her cheeks redden. 'We just went riding.'

'Aw, come on Pru,' said Lew, flicking her cheek with a show of familiarity. 'I asked you out good and proper and now I'll finish what I started. I'm responsible for you, darlin'.' His smile was far too warm and his wink endorsed the lie.

He was laying it on thick. Pru wished he wouldn't. Flynn's mood was growing blacker by the minute.

'You haven't done a good job looking after her so far,' he said crushingly.

'But I can at least get her home and safely tucked into bed.'

The muscle in Flynn's cheek ticked and clenched at the mention of bed. He seared Lew and Prudence with a furious glare. 'Well, you'd best get going then. Who am I to keep you from your bed,' he said with steely menace. 'I shan't detain you any longer.' He then turned on his heel and stalked out of the room, slamming the door behind him with such a force the sash windows rattled.

Pru wanted to burst into tears. It must be the aftershock of the fall, because why else would she want to cry? And why did she suddenly feel so bereft?

'That went well,' said Lew. His inappropriate jauntiness cauterised her desire to cry. Now she wanted to brain someone. Preferably Lew!

'You think it did?'

'Absolutely. Flynn doesn't know what's hit him.'

'He's more likely to do the hitting, the state he's in,' she said dryly. 'I think you'd better get me home before he comes back and fires you on the spot.'

9

'Need cheering up again, babe?' asked Toni bringing a cup of tea into the small sleep-out bedroom where Pru was resting on the saggy single bed. It was three days since her accident. Lew had rung daily to check on her, but she'd heard zilch from Flynn. This should have pleased her. It was what she'd wanted, wasn't it? But instead, she found his silence depressing.

On top of that, the urge to cry hadn't lessened, even though the shock of the fall had receded. She was very, very low.

'What did you have in mind?' she asked Toni listlessly as she stared at the cracked and stained ceiling and morosely counted the handful of geckos for the zillionth time.

'Blue.'

'Blue?' She frowned, half-heartedly

trying to keep up with Toni's erratic conversation.

'Dye. I found this big bottle of blue food colouring in the storeroom the other day and it's just begging to be used.'

'For what?'

'Babe — your hair! What else would you use it for?'

Pru shook her head tiredly. 'I don't know, Toni. I'm not in the mood.'

'It'll put a smile on your face.'

'No it won't. It would just match my mood.'

'Horse-feathers.'

'Toni! I've told you before. Do not mention horses in my hearing.'

'Sorry. But you've gotta do this, babe. The dye will cheer us both up.'

'You don't need cheering up. You're upbeat enough for the two of us.'

'Do it for me.'

'Aw, Toni . . . '

'That's settled then.'

'I haven't agreed to anything!' Pru said indignantly.

Toni laughed. 'Come on, babe, live a little.'

It was enough to make a grown woman weep because that was exactly what Pru was trying to do, though very badly in her opinion.

★   ★   ★

The dye was used but Pru's hair didn't turn blue when Toni did her stuff. Instead, it went purple.

'Guess we should have realised blue on pink would turn purple.' Toni tilted her head to one side and pursed her lips. 'But it's a beaut look all the same.' She grinned at Jimmy, seeking his approval.

The three of them were in the bar ready for the rush of the early evening customers and Jimmy was trying his best not to pull a shocked face. He didn't want to upset his girls, especially Pru who'd been so depressed.

'It's certainly different, love,' he said diplomatically. 'And it does suit you . . .

in a sort of bohemian way.'

'And it blends nicely with the bruises,' added Toni for good measure.

'But I don't feel any happier,' confessed Pru. The thrill of changing her hair colour had palled. What was the big deal? How pathetic she'd been thinking dyeing her hair would make her feel different inside.

'I know,' said Toni with blithe confidence of a body-piercing maniac, 'maybe you need some earrings to add to those minuscule bourgeois studs of yours. I'll go get my kit.'

'No! No more needles!' But Toni had already gone. For a big woman, Pru thought glumly, she moved extremely fast.

Toni came back into the bar with her little red suitcase stuffed full of the tricks of her tattoo and piercing trade. With a flourish, she drew out a blue pen.

Pru had expected something far worse than a pen. At the very least a twelve-inch needle or a cutthroat razor with a glinting, honed edge. But a pen? 'What's that for?' she asked with puzzled innocence.

'To mark where the holes are to go. So where do you want them, babe?' Toni asked, a zealous light alive in her eyes.

That was enough for Prudence. She took one look at the kit and everything went black.

*   *   *

'Pru! Pru? Honey, can you hear me?'

Flynn? Every time she was out cold she heard his voice. She was obsessed!

'Pru?'

As the mists cleared she realised perhaps she wasn't imagining his voice. That he was actually by her side.

She then discovered she was sitting on the floor. And not just sitting, as if at a Sunday school picnic.

Oh no!

Her head was thrust between her bare knees. She tried to jerk her head up and pull her knees together in one swift manoeuvre. She didn't want everyone and his dog getting an eyeful. But a strong hand stayed firmly on the back of her neck, preventing her from pulling back.

'What the hell happened? Get the nurse! Fetch Joannie,' yelled Flynn. 'She's suffering complications from her accident. She needs a doctor.'

'Cool it, Flynn.' Toni sounded as if something was amusing her greatly. 'She conked out because of the thought of needles. She's such a wuss.'

'Needles?'

'I was going to pierce her. You know, to cheer her up.'

'Piercings make people happy?' said Flynn. Pru reckoned he was right to sound so doubtful. He didn't know the half of it where Toni was concerned.

'It does me,' said Toni and Pru thought, for the six millionth time, the woman should be certified.

'Goodness,' said Flynn in fascinated amazement. 'And you wanted to be pierced, Amaryllis?'

Pru mumbled a negative, her head still stuck between her knees.

'As I said, she's a wuss,' chuckled Toni.

At that moment the phone rang for Jimmy and he called to Toni to oversee the cooking.

'Gotta go, kids,' said Toni.

'And not a moment too soon,' grumbled Pru.

'I heard that, babe. Good job I don't insult easily.' She laughed again. 'I'm in the kitchen if you need me.'

Flynn and Pru were now alone. Pru didn't think it was a big improvement on her day. Embarrassment and humiliation prickled her skin in equal amounts.

'Pru, honey, are you okay?'

Pru swatted at his hand. 'I would be if you'd let me up for air.'

'You had me worried there for a minute,' he said as his hand dropped to her shoulder. Pru's head snapped up. Stars exploded behind her eyeballs and she breathed deeply to disperse them.

'Whoa! The room's still spinning. Just give me a moment.'

'Does your head hurt?'

'No, it's fine.' Actually it thudded like a malfunctioning jackhammer, but she didn't want to tell Flynn that. He might hike her off to his precious Joannie at the hospital and she'd already filled Pru with tetanus needles and such.

'Let's get you to the nurse to make sure.'

'No!' she squeaked. 'It's not the accident causing my fainting. It was Toni's fault. I can't abide needles but she was insisting I'd feel better if she'd put a couple more studs in my ears.' She shuddered. 'That woman needs serious therapy.'

'I'd feel more relaxed if we took you for a check-up with Joannie,' Flynn said with gruff concern.

'But I wouldn't. She's a sadist, that woman. And a bully. Just leave me be. I'll be okay. I just need a bit of time to clear my head.'

'But you could be suffering from delayed shock after your fall.'

'I'm not! Joannie's already checked. A zillion times. Now stop bullying me!' She let her bottom lip quiver ever so slightly.

The ruse worked.

'Okay, okay. You win. I'll back off.' But Flynn didn't look pleased about it. He scooped her off the floor and settled into a chair with Pru on his lap. 'But you had me rattled,' he muttered.

He had her rattled too, especially doing that.

'Don't fuss. I'll be okay,' she said tetchily.

'I damn well hope so.' There was a wealth of meaning behind his statement.

Pru raised her head and regarded Flynn. He stared steadily back at her.

'You tie me in knots, Ms Stark. It'll be a relief when you finally leave Ibis Springs.'

Pru's mouth dropped open in surprise. What had happened to the man who'd wanted to have an affair with her only days before? Now, suddenly, he wanted her gone? Had her pseudo date with Lew put him off?

Even though she'd decided to leave Ibis Springs herself, she was perversely annoyed he wanted her to go too.

'I thought you wanted me to stay,' she snapped.

'That was before I knew you were . . . you know . . . '

'What? A virgin?'

'I don't want to disappoint you.'

'But I've got nothing to compare you with!'

'Thank you for your vote of confidence but I didn't mean in bed.' He gave a rueful laugh, which lacked his characteristic warmth and humour.

'So what do you mean?'

'I can't offer you more than an affair and you deserve so much more than that.'

'Believe me, I'd be happy with just an affair.' She conveniently forgot her resolution not to be naked with him, to keep her tattoo under wraps. Golly, maybe she did have concussion!

'Well, it won't be with me, sweetheart. My conscience wouldn't allow it.' He frowned slightly, his mouth twisting. 'Anyway, you've changed your tune. Before I went away you said you didn't want a relationship with me.' He gave her a quizzical look. 'Why the change of heart?'

'It's a woman's prerogative to change her mind.' And hers had just seesawed right back to where she'd started with him, except she wanted him even more badly than before. Toni had been right. Flynn was worth fighting for. They deserved a fling.

'Well, I've changed mine too.'

'You're not allowed to,' she huffed indignantly.

'Why not?'

'Because you're not a woman.'

'I could charge you with discrimination.'

Pru waved her hand dismissively. 'Reconsider, Flynn. It would be so much fun to have an affair.' Crikey, did she actually say that? Prudence, the boring stick-in-the-mud, depressingly naive, primary school teacher? She *had* come a long way since London, and not just in kilometres.

'It would. I don't doubt it for one second. But Pru, I gave it a lot of thought while I was in Perth and I believe I'm doing the right thing.'

He paused.

'Why do you wear such skimpy things and keep dyeing your hair?' he suddenly asked.

She stared at his large, tanned hand resting on her thigh and sighed. 'Because it's fun and adventurous,' she said stoically. 'Not boring.' She explained further. 'Exciting.'

'Excuse me?'

'Like an affair would be. With you. But you wouldn't understand.' Pru was perturbed that her voice wobbled. She hoped Flynn hadn't noticed.

The seesaw had dipped right, right down to rock bottom. She wanted

Flynn to love her unconditionally, just so that once in her life she would be able to experience glorious, passionate loving and not be sidelined as boring.

'You're a sweet girl,' he said, looping a purple strand of hair behind her ear. 'I wish things could be different between us.'

'So do I. You wouldn't reconsider?' she asked with empty hope.

'Oh Prudence.'

'I'll take that as a no.' And she slid off his knee and walked out of the bar, not once glancing back.

10

Flynn was going mad.

So much for his good intentions to keep Amaryllis at arm's length. All he wanted to do was drag her close and kiss her senseless each and every time he saw her. Which was often, now she'd taken to hanging out with Lew.

She'd even been brave enough — or stupid enough — to have more riding lessons on Dolores, though she was no natural horsewoman. She had fallen off several times and Flynn was dead scared she'd break something. When he'd tried to remonstrate with her, she'd shot back that life was there to be lived to the full and if she killed herself doing something exciting it was nobody's business but her own.

Prudence demonstrated a glorious passion for life. Flynn envied her the passion and enjoyment she seemed to have. It made his own existence look boring and dull. Maybe his solitary life was an empty martyrdom? Perhaps he could chill out more and include someone special in his world? Relax his unwritten rule to reinvent the station regardless. Because at the end of the day, what did he have? A beautiful, functioning, profitable property for just one person. There'd be no one to share it with. No one to pass it on to . . .

And here he was, once again staring out the study window and witnessing the easy camaraderie that existed between Pru and Lew and feeling as sick as a lovelorn teenager. It made him fume because it could have been him down there teaching her to ride and not his station manager. And he was the only one to blame. Pru had offered him the chance of love and he'd turned her down. What an idiot.

His temper wasn't helped by the fact she was looking so utterly desirable. The fresh air and exertion had brought a rosy glow to her cheeks and a sparkle to her eyes. Her tight jeans fitted her like a second skin. Her old T-shirt clung damply to her curves. And her delighted giggles made him feel excluded, and emphasised his stark, lone status.

Flynn was jealous and he was finding it a bitter experience. But he wasn't the only one suffering. Rachel was too.

She'd just slammed out the office, bang in the middle of their business meeting, with her usual cool composure rattled and aggravated by the sight of Pru and Lew fooling around. She'd muttered something about all men being fools and Flynn had to agree with her, because he was the biggest fool out.

But however crazy he felt, Flynn knew he was doing the best thing keeping away from Prudence. He'd thought long and hard while he'd been away from Ibis Springs and knew he'd made the right decision.

He'd been intrigued when he'd first realised Pru was a virgin, but then cold reality had hit. How could he make love to her and then just walk away? Because he would walk away, of that he was certain. His cattle station came first. It had to. Which meant they would both have ended up losers.

Pru was inexperienced and sweet. He knew he was being selfish, but he didn't want to open himself up to the pain of loving a woman who might, just might — especially with Prudence's crazy fads and volatile fashions — love him and then leave him just like those women had done to his father. Such a risk wasn't in his scheme of things. He'd vowed after his father's third divorce and bitter lawsuit never to marry. It had been easy to keep to the master plan.

Until now.

Until Amaryllis had burst into his life and turned it upside down and inside out. He was even beginning to question how much he cared for the land. Did it mean more to him than this feisty, sexy woman who tugged at his heartstrings and plagued his dreams?

Every time he saw her, his resolve

crumbled a little more.

There was only one thing to do — not see her at all. Perhaps then he'd begin to be objective and stick to his dream of making Ibis Springs Station the best in the state.

★   ★   ★

Pru had to kiss Flynn Maguire.

As having a full-blown affair obviously wasn't going to happen due to his high moral stance, she might as well settle for at least one proper kiss.

This obsession to kiss Flynn had been simmering for days now, and Pru reckoned it was time for action. The only problem was how to go about it. Flynn was proving to be a difficult man to pin down.

He was avoiding her, still hung up about her virginal status. Goodness, the man's chivalry was driving her loopy. Pru chewed the inside of her cheek and thought hard. There had to be a way of getting him to come into town.

Her gaze fell on the big pile of mail behind the counter.

Now there was an idea . . .

The backlog of mail had come through on the buses, which had been running for a couple of days now. Pru had been tempted to hop on one and leave Ibis Springs in a cloud of red dust and no regrets. But when the crunch had come, she couldn't bring herself to leave. Because there would be regrets. Or one big one.

Because she hadn't yet kissed the Mighty Flynn.

And she would kiss him, even if she achieved nothing else.

Pru contemplated the huge stack of parcels ready for collection. Hmm. It was worth a shot. And it had to be today because she was in sole charge of the place. Jimmy and Toni were away for the afternoon, catching up on some R & R.

Before she could chicken out, Pru snatched up the phone and punched in Flynn's number. She held her breath while the phone rang. It rang and rang. Darn, he wasn't there. The bubble of excitement, which had formed in her belly at the thought of seeing Flynn, began to deflate. But it fired up again, as if pumped with neat helium, when he suddenly answered, sounding breath-less.

'Hi,' Pru said, immediately feeling breathless herself.

'Yes?' She could hear him sucking in air. He'd obviously run for the phone.

'You have a parcel here,' she said.

'Lew can pick it up when he's next in.'

Pru crossed her fingers. 'It says urgent. Would you like me to bring it over to the station?'

Silence pulsed between them. 'No.' He was curt, almost rude. Or was it panic? She almost giggled.

'What is it?' he asked. 'Any ideas?'

'I don't know. It's quite big . . . '

'But I haven't ordered anything.'

'Well, it might be a present. Really, Flynn, I don't mind bringing it over.'

'No! I'll come and get it. Thanks.' He broke the connection and Pru frowned down at the receiver. He'd probably spit chips when he realised just what the present was. In fact, it wasn't much of a present.

Flynn was there within the hour.

'Where's the package?' he said, tipping his hat at her as he strode into the bar looking big and blond and dishevelled. His jeans were grubby, his shirt not much better and his boots were so dusty it was hard to see what their actual colour was. But all in all, he looked absolutely gorgeous.

Pru's pulse rate kicked up into a rollicking tattoo that did nothing for her nerves.

At the same time, her mouth went dry.

Could she do this? Did she have the courage? Was she brazen enough?

There was only one way to find out . . .

'Hi, Flynn, long time no see. How are you?' she managed to squeak out, trying unsuccessfully for a nonchalant note. She sounded desperately anxious to her own ears but hopefully not to his.

'Fine.' He didn't elaborate. Didn't even make eye contact, which didn't bode well.

'Good . . . ' She cast around for something, anything to say, as he wasn't going to loosen up and make things easy for her. In fact he looked as tightly coiled as she felt. 'Been up to much?' she asked inanely.

'No. Yes. Look, Prudence, I haven't got much time. Where's this package?' He was regarding her warily, which did little for her self-confidence.

It was now or never.

'Here.' Pru grabbed the hem of her T-shirt and hiked up the lime green material. Across her stomach was a red and white sticky label sporting the legend URGENT.

Flynn froze as his eyes fixed on the word. He swallowed visibly.

'You're the urgent package?'

'It is urgent. I want you to kiss me.

221

Now.' It came out in a rush, the words tumbling over themselves in her effort to get them out before she fluffed it and chickened out.

'You lied to get me over here just so you could to tell me that?' His voice rose with accusation. A muscle ticked in his cheek. His eyes darkened dangerously.

'It's not a lie. I'm the present. Sort of.' She tugged back down her T-shirt, feeling more than a little silly. So much for good ideas.

'Saints preserve me!' He sounded hoarse. Disbelieving. She couldn't blame him. She could hardly believe she was doing this herself.

'Well, would you have come over otherwise?' she said in a small voice.

'No.' He shook his head, dazed.

'There you go then.' She began to feel more confident. 'I knew you'd been avoiding me. So, I repeat, I want you to kiss me.'

'But why?' It was a plea for understanding.

Pru huffed. 'What a stupid question.'

She stepped around from the bar and marched up to Flynn as if she meant business, which she did. He took a step back. She advanced two and grabbed his shirt. 'Please Flynn,' she urged. 'I made a decision weeks ago to live more adventurously. Because my self-confidence took a hammering. So today I want to be adventurous and kiss an Aussie cowboy. Indulge me. Please.'

'I don't know about this living adventurously lark. It seems to cause a heap of trouble.' He prised her fingers loose and held her at arm's length.

'You don't need to know anything about it. But it's important to me. Please, trust me, Flynn. I only want a kiss.'

'Nothing is ever 'only' with you, Prudence Stark. Your parents didn't name you very well. You don't have a prudent bone in your body.'

Actually she did. She was prudent through and through, right to the very marrow, and would still be exercising the boring virtue of prudence if Dean hadn't done his dumping routine.

But Flynn didn't need to know any of that. It was on a purely need-to-know basis.

'Well, you can call me anything you like as long as you kiss me. Please?' Pru held her breath as Flynn took off his akubra and dragged his hand through his bleached blond hair. That was a good sign, she decided. He was rattled but he was thinking about it. Pru suspended her breath for several long seconds. She willed him to do it, to kiss her and be damned. He scowled down at her and she almost giggled, he looked so stern.

'This is not a good idea,' he said finally, expelling a big breath.

'Let me be the judge of that.' She swayed slightly towards him, inviting him to join her.

'You don't understand.' He was fighting a rearguard action. He knew it; she knew it. The deal was almost done.

'It's just a kiss, Flynn. No strings

attached. I'll be leaving here in a couple of days now the bus strike is over. And no one need know about it.' Did she sound too wheedling? Was she laying it on too thick?

'Why me?' he ground out with a certain amount of bewilderment.

Because I fancy you rotten.

But she didn't dare say that or he'd balk big time and she was ever so close to her wish. So she said instead, 'Availability and I know you won't take advantage. You've already told me you don't want an affair. So I reckon you'll just kiss me and that will be that.'

It sounded oh so simple.

'Christ! I'm only human.' His admission seemed to be dragged up from the very depths of his soul, which made Pru glad.

'Stop talking and get on with it. Someone might turn up any minute and then we won't be able to do it.'

'Pru . . . '

But Pru was already tilting up her face for his kiss. She closed her eyes and puckered her lips.

Nothing.

She waited.

Still nothing.

Pru cranked open an eye. Flynn was staring at her. He seemed mesmerised. She snapped open her other eye and planted her hands on her hips. 'Flynn . . . '

'Okay, okay.' Almost trance-like, he reached for her, pulling her close so she could feel the heat of his body through the thin fabric of her shirt. Slowly he lowered his head until his mouth was an inch away from hers. He hesitated and it was Pru who closed the distance between them, planting her mouth firmly over his so he was in no doubt about what she wanted.

At first his lips were warm and gentle, moulding against hers in exquisite discovery.

It was a slow and sultry kiss.

So this was what it was like to kiss a cowboy.

Pru sighed and brought up her hand

to cup the back of his head and pull him deeper into the embrace. It was good, so very good. But it wasn't enough! She was hungry for more and was sure it was there for the taking.

She raised herself on tiptoe for an even snugger fit. Her lips firmer on his, her small breasts squashed against his muscular torso, their thighs kissing as well as their mouths. Heat rippled through her right to the tips of her orange painted toenails.

Now this was more potent than a dozen Balinese cocktails.

This was more heart-thumping than riding an out-of-control Dolores at full gallop.

This was . . . absolute heaven.

Pru gave another blissful sigh and then tentatively touched Flynn's tongue with hers.

Whoosh!

Suddenly Flynn was meeting her with a fierce onslaught of his own. His hands cupped her bottom, his thumbs skimming the swell of her buttocks that were barely covered by the lurid, stretchy orange micro skirt. He lifted her off the ground, and, without breaking the kiss, carried her over to one of the tables. Her foot caught a rogue chair on the way. It crashed to the ground but neither of them paid it any attention, they were too intent on kissing.

Flynn slid her on to the table, nudging her legs apart to allow him to get closer. Pru's legs entwined around him, pinning him to her core. She could feel him hard against her. Her own body responded like a lightning strike. Fire scorched through her veins. Her chest swelled as her heart pounded in rapid rhythm.

But it was Flynn who groaned and deepened the kiss.

Pru half opened her eyes and saw his were tightly closed, his face flushed with a sheen of perspiration that gave his olive skin a rich, deep lustre. He looked like an ancient god: golden and perfect. She shivered with a need she'd never experienced before and realised, in a flash of panic, she was way out of her depth.

Flynn pushed her backwards on to the table, his body weight holding her down so he could use his lips and tongue and teeth to greater effect. Pru was spiralling with sensations she'd only ever read about in back issues of Cosmopolitan when waiting at the dentist's surgery.

If Flynn carried on like this, she'd melt into a pool of overwhelming sensation. And it scared the stuffing out of her!

Flynn was leaning so far over her, Pru could barely breathe. He pulled her arms above her head and held them easily in one hand. With the other he swept down the side of her body. Her lime green top had ridden up. Her snazzy short skirt had done the same. There was too much bare flesh for Pru to feel secure. Especially as Flynn had found it all and was causing her to goosebump deliciously as his fingertips roved over her.

And still he carried on kissing her. Whoever had said that men couldn't do more than one thing at a time didn't know Flynn!

Pru might have initiated all this, but she'd given up leading the way once Flynn's tongue had joined the action and his hands had slipped under her skirt. Because she knew she was lost, lost en route to somewhere she'd never been before. Sure, there were signposts: rapid heart, rapid pulse, rapid breathing. But she didn't know if she should go there. She felt like a babe in the wood. There should be manuals about the dangers of kissing like this.

It was all too much.

If her heart went any faster it would rock out of her body. And if she couldn't suck in much needed oxygen, then that was it, she'd be dead in paradise. Hey, but what a way to go!

But no, things had to stop. And now before it was too late!

But how?

The only way was for her to regain control. She buried her fingers into the thick golden thatch of his hair and yanked hard.

'Yeow!'

Flynn released her mouth. She greedily sucked in air.

'What'd you do that for?' Flynn rubbed his head. He was still leaning over her, squashing her flat against the formica tabletop.

★　★　★

Because I was suffocating through desire and lack of oxygen.

But she couldn't say that. She was far too rattled.

'I'd had enough,' she managed to force out through passion-throbbing lips.

'Oh,' Flynn was stunned at her admission. 'But we've only just started.'

'Just started?'

Good grief! There was more?

'I thought we were warming up nicely.'

Warming up? But that was a blazing inferno! What would it be like if he really got going?

She flashed with heat just thinking about it.

'I've got work to do,' she hastily improvised, knowing full well any further kissing would be the death of her.

'Work?' He took his weight on his hands, his arms locked straight either side of Pru. She was feeling decidedly disadvantaged, lying there with her clothes askew, hair probably matching, and her tingling lips feeling swollen to double their normal size. She resisted the urge to touch them with her tongue to see if they were. She didn't want to start Flynn off again and the way he was staring at her, it wouldn't take an ace Mensa student to know he was primed for more action. A lot more. Just the thought of him doing any more to her made her feel dizzyingly light-headed.

No, she really couldn't handle it.

'Well, thanks for that, Flynn,' said Pru, wriggling off the table and slipping out from under his arm. She tugged her clothes back in place and smoothed back her purple hair, hoping he didn't notice her trembling hands. 'At least I can now say I've kissed an Aussie cowboy. I'm truly grateful.' She was glad she sounded quite normal and calm, because inside she was all jellied with desire.

'Grateful?' Flynn's jaw dropped and he slowly straightened up from the table.

'Appreciative.' Pru bit the side of her mouth to stop her sudden urge to laugh. Flynn was acting as if he'd been poleaxed.

'Appreciative?'

'Yup. Now I really do need to get on. Jimmy's left me this huge list of jobs to do.'

'I don't believe it,' said Flynn, dangerous sparks exploding in his eyes. 'You drive me crazy for days on end, romping about the place with Lew and wearing clothes designed to slay every man in Christendom. You get me over here on false pretences so you can try out your seduction routine. And then you have the gall to walk away!'

'That was not a seduction routine. That was merely a kiss.' She prudently ignored his jibe about Lew, because she felt justified helping the station manager win Rachel's heart.

As for her clothes, Flynn might just be right about those and so she ignored that dig too. 'Be seeing you, Flynn. And thanks.' She hurriedly left the room before she spoilt the effect by giggling.

★   ★   ★

Flynn watched her go. Of course, he could go after her and kiss her senseless. It wouldn't take much persuasion to have her back and tangoing in his arms again. She'd been right along with him during that explosive kiss, enjoying it and responding to it just like him.

Flynn shook his head. He'd known she'd be dynamite if he allowed himself to touch her. Yes sir. Powerful dynamite, with extra packed poundage that flared on impact.

And now the damage was done.

Surprise.

And he wanted to kiss her again.

Surprise, surprise!

And some.

Dammit, it was going to be even harder trying to keep away from Prudence Stark, if not impossible after that kiss.

He watched the swing doors close behind her and debated whether or not to go after her. Best not, he decided ruefully, resolutely squashing down the immediate bloom of regret.

Because the woman was trouble, with a capital T, and he had a station to run.

11

'You're looking a little flushed, darling Prudence!' It was Lew and he had a wicked, all-too-knowing smile on his face. He was propped up against a counter in the kitchen as Pru burst through the swing doors, zinging on high octane after her scorcher of a kiss.

She jumped, shocked. She'd been expecting to have the kitchen to herself. Had banked on it so she could cool down and try and regain her shattered composure. If Flynn hadn't been in the bar, she'd have high-tailed it out of the kitchen. But Flynn was there and there was no way on earth she was ready to confront him again. So she was stuck. She'd have to face Lew and get it over with.

'I'm hot,' she stated. Hot in more ways than she cared to admit, to Lew or herself! She snatched up an old magazine from the sideboard and began fanning herself with frantic, small motions. 'Where did you spring from all of a sudden?'

'Well, I was going into the bar for a drink, but I saw you were . . . er . . . busy, so I decided to slip in here instead. At least until it was safe to enter the bar without the threat of third-degree burns.'

'Oh Lord. You saw.' Pru said, mortified. So much for secret kisses. Had anyone else seen them making out on the table? It'd be all around Ibis Springs before sundown.

Lew rolled his eyes and grinned. 'Sure did. Phew, if I'd been wearing spectacles they'd have steamed up good and proper at the view!'

Pru turned her back on him, threw down the magazine and began banging about the pots and pans. The action and noise was a ruse. She wasn't doing anything constructive with the cookware but she needed to buy time to cool and calm down, gather her scattered, embarrassed thoughts and quieten her erratic pulse rate.

Lew chuckled at her consternation. 'That was quite a scene going on in there,' he said. 'Definitely 'R' rated. Phew-ee, I'm amazed there's any paint left on them there walls after that scorcher.'

So he wasn't going to let it drop. Great. Just what she needed, to be remind of those incredible sizzling moments, but at least her heart rhythm was beginning to revert to its normal speed.

She shrugged with a nonchalance she was far from feeling and then crashed the pans about a bit more, just for good measure. 'But for all the outward display of passion played out on the table in there, it didn't really achieve anything,' she said, unaware the wistfulness in her voice was a dead giveaway.

'Did you want it to?'

'Maybe. Perhaps. I don't know.'

'I'm curious. What did you think it would achieve, kissing in full view in a public place and all?'

Pru stopped fiddling with the saucepan and was silent. What had really been behind her hell-bent scheme to kiss Flynn? Had it been a deep down desire to show him there was something special between them? To make a difference? Show him she cared?

'It's not like you were expecting the full works, being in broad daylight,' carried on Lew.

Pru flushed. No, she certainly hadn't anticipated the rapid freefall into hot need.

'Unless you're into extrovert sex?'

'No!' she squeaked in protest. 'I didn't expect so much . . . reaction,' she confessed.

'Do you love him, Pru?'

She shivered as his softly spoken suggestion hit a chord. 'Love? No!' She was quick to deny it. She was on the rebound. Nothing else. Love took time. Like months. Years. And it took courage, which she didn't have much of.

No, no way was she in love with Flynn.

But golly, what if she was? Or Flynn thought so? He'd head for the hills at breakneck speed and she'd never see him again. His priority was to the station, not his heart and he wouldn't compromise. He'd told her that. Rachel had told her that. She knew it for a fact.

'I'm not in love.'

But Lew wasn't fooled. He rolled his eyes again and said, 'Are you sure? You were steaming out there like a Turkish bath.'

'Oh really,' she tried to laugh it off but her voice cracked.

'Pru, 'fess up. You're as hung up on Maguire as I am on Rachel.'

'No. Yes. Well, okay, maybe a bit. But it's probably more lust. And how the hell am I to tell the difference? I just want the man,' she almost wailed.

'I'm happy to help you sort out the difference here and now.'

'How?' She frowned at him.

'I have a plan,' he said and grinned as

he moved towards her. He prized the cooking pots from her hands and placed them on the counter. His next action took her completely by surprise, because he then engulfed her in a suffocating bear hug.

'Lew,' she squealed, half giggling and pushing against his wiry frame, wondering what he was doing.

'Shut up and join in the experiment,' he said and then kissed her full and hard on the lips before she could realise his intention.

Pru was too stunned to react, though a portion of her brain acknowledged he was all male. He was lean and hard and definitely knew how to kiss a girl thoroughly.

He deepened the kiss and Pru let him, though she felt no urge to join in as she had with Flynn. Perhaps Lew's kiss would wipe out the longing for Flynn . . .

Faint hope!

He let her go after a few moments, his hands resting on the swell of her hips. 'So?' he said.

'So?' she echoed stupidly.

'So what do you think? Was my kiss on a par with kissing Maguire?'

'It was nice.'

Even as she said it, Pru knew 'nice' was faint praise and she cringed. Yes, his kiss was nice. And pleasant. And warming. And she'd probably learn to enjoy and respond to it. If she wanted to. But — and it was a big, big but — there were no bells or sirens going off. No rapid heartbeats. No molten fire in the blood stream. No deep desperation for more as she'd experienced with Flynn.

'Just nice?'

'Yes. Quite pleasant, in fact. Not horrible at all.' Keep digging, Pru!

'Ouch.'

'Sorry.'

'S'okay. So not earth-shattering, eh?'

'No. Warm and fuzzy rather than earth-shattering. Sorry.' Why on earth did she keep apologising? She wasn't the one asking to be kissed by him. 'But it was . . . er . . . nice.'

'And you wouldn't mind being kissed by me again?'

'Only on the right occasions, like Christmas and birthdays,' she answered honestly.

'Guess it wasn't just lust out there in the café, then.'

'Guess not.'

'Which means it must be love.' He flicked her cheek and then he focused on something over her left shoulder. 'Uh-oh,' he said. 'The big boss man himself. Hi, Flynn.'

Flynn? Flynn! He was here? She thought he'd have been long gone after their steamy encounter. Guess not. How much has he witnessed? Oh lordy!

Pru spun around, almost falling over herself in her haste. Yup, it was Flynn all right and he was acting as cranky as a hungry tiger faced with only a pile of bleached, buzzard-picked bones for his supper.

'What is this? Kissing as many cowboys as you can in a cool five minutes?' He growled. His scowl contorted his beautiful face and Pru yearned to reach out to him, tell him he'd made a mistake, that it had been Lew kissing her, not the other way round. But he wouldn't believe her anyway. He was too wound up and mad. He'd probably bite!

'I can kiss whom I like,' she said, fronting up to him, deciding attack was the best form of defence under the circumstances. 'There's no law against it.'

'I thought you were different from other women, Prudence. You disappoint me.'

Her heart cracked.

Lew coughed apologetically. 'There's been a misunderstanding, boss,' he said with a lopsided smile at odds with the wary look in his eyes. He was watching those fists too, Pru realised. 'That kiss was nothing serious.'

'Oh really. It looked pretty full on to me,' Flynn ground out.

'Nah, we were just fooling about.'

'Which you've been doing a lot of lately. I sometimes wonder what I pay you for,' Flynn snapped.

'There's no need to get angry with Lew. We have a perfectly good reason for carrying on like we do,' said Pru doing her hands on hips routine. She wasn't going to tell him about Rachel. That was Lew's business and nothing to do with Flynn.

'I'm sure you have. Notches on the bedpost?'

'For goodness' sake, it's not like that. We haven't done anything wrong. My relationship with Lew is perfectly innocent.'

'I know what I saw, Prudence.'

'If that's what you want to believe, then fine. I'm out of here in a couple of days anyway. I've had my fill of Ibis Springs and its infuriating men.' She jabbed a finger in the middle of his chest so he wouldn't be in any doubt over which particular man she meant.

'Great. Go. And it won't be a moment too soon.' He grabbed the jabbing hand and held it tightly in his own.

Pru had the crazy feeling he was going to yank her towards him and kiss her again, even though he was spitting tacks the size of rail irons. But the moment was lost as someone knocked delicately on the door.

The three of them turned in unison towards the door.

'Ah, here you all are.' Rachel Burnley was standing there looking cool and neat in spite of the humidity of the day. She was wearing ice-blue cotton trousers and a close fitting white tank top. A slight smile played around her lips, which were coated with a mere hint of pale pink lipstick. She was the mistress of understated chic while Pru glumly felt the opposite in her sweaty, tacky lime green and orange get-up and frizzy purple hair. She should never attempt comparisons with that woman. She would lose every time.

Rachel regarded them all with faint

amusement. 'Well, well. Quite a little party,' she said.

Pru yanked her hand away from Flynn. 'Hello, Rachel,' she said, breaking through the crackling tension of the small kitchen. 'Are you after a drink?' She wiped her sweating hands on the sheer material of her skirt and bustled towards the bar, unaware of Flynn's tortured expression as his eyes followed her movements.

'I wouldn't say no to an iced tea,' remarked Rachel, stepping to one side to let Pru pass.

'You guys having one?' asked Pru, tossing the question over her shoulder, hoping to avoid eye contact with either of them.

She needn't have worried. They weren't planning on hanging around. In fact, they were just about running out of the door, Flynn making it terribly clear he and Lew had work to do.

'I'll catch you later,' he said to Rachel, ignoring Pru completely. 'Let's get moving Lew, we've wasted enough time here already.'

'I'm sorry if I interrupted anything important,' murmured Rachel, daintily sipping her drink. Her face was as smoothly bland as usual but Pru detected an underlying layer of permafrost.

Because she was leaving soon, it was now or never, Pru decided. She had to help Lew with his dream.

'Flynn was in a rage because he caught me kissing Lew,' she said airily and monitored Rachel's shocked reaction out of the corner of her eye.

Rachel brought the glass of iced tea down with a loud crack on the counter. Her lips clamped tight together but she didn't utter a word.

Pru decided to provoke her some more. 'And he was mad because I've been spending so much time in Lew's company, what with our horse riding lessons and mucking about with the karaoke machine.'

'His anger is justified,' said Rachel with a snap. Her lips thinned into a hard, uncompromising line. 'You don't seem to be content with hooking Flynn. You appear to want every man in the district dancing to your tune. It's sickening to watch them fawning over you.'

'I'm not interested in all the men,' Pru protested with self-righteous indignation.

Rachel ignored her. 'I warned you before about Flynn, but why Lew too? It's so unfair.'

'On whom?'

Rachel hesitated. 'On both of them,' she said.

Pru took a deep breath and jumped in with both feet. 'Which one does it hurt most to see me with?' she asked gently.

'Which . . . ?'

'That's right, Rachel. Which of those two men would you prefer I dropped?'

'What do you mean?' The woman sounded incensed.

'You can't have both of them. That's unfair, as you rightly pointed out to me.

But I'm only attracted to one of them. What about you?'

'I . . . How dare you! That's my business.'

'Do something about it, Rachel, before it's too late. You're fond of Flynn. You like who he is and what he stands for. But what about Lew? Did you like seeing me carrying on with him at the station? Was it nice to know I'd kissed him in the kitchen only seconds ago? And I've kissed Flynn too. How does that make you feel?'

'Why are you saying all this?' Rachel's voice shook with outrage. 'What's the point?'

'Because I'm leaving Ibis Springs. It doesn't matter to me who you choose, but it matters to those two men. I suggest you follow your heart, not your head. There's too much happiness at stake to marry for the wrong reason. A lump of dirt — okay, Ibis Springs Station is a big lump of dirt — is no comparison to the love of a good man. And Lew is a very good man who loves you deeply. There, I've said my piece. Do what you have to do. It's all the same to me.'

Rachel stared at Pru, wide-eyed and taut, for several seconds and then suddenly her shoulders relaxed. She slumped forward slightly and dipped her finger in the condensation of the glass, absently drawing a heart on the counter top.

'I've hated seeing you with Lew,' she admitted softly. 'It made me feel sick to my stomach.'

'Good. That's what we hoped.'

Rachel's head snapped up and she stared at Pru. 'Excuse me?'

'Lew and I decided we'd try and make you jealous. He's loved you for the longest time, Rachel, but didn't think he stood a chance.'

'But why? Why didn't he say anything?'

'Because of Flynn — who he is and what he is and what that means to you. Lew's no fool. He knows what's important to you: the land and breeding. Flynn has both.'

'Flynn? I suppose so. As I told you before, I always thought we'd make a go of it one day. Never thought anything different.'

'But Flynn's determined not to marry. He wants to protect his precious station from the designs of gold-digging women.' Pru was unable to keep the bitterness from creeping into her voice.

Rachel sighed. 'I know that's what he says. But it's only because of his father. Jonas Maguire was always a sucker for a pretty face. Flynn hated all the different women, the upheavals and financial strain. But I've always thought he'd get fed up living alone and realise I didn't want him for his money. We're a perfect match, with our similar backgrounds and interests.'

'Hah. You'll be waiting forever. I think he's a lost cause,' said Pru.

'Perhaps you're right.' Rachel gave Pru an assessing stare. 'I can live with it, but I'm sorry for you. Perhaps you care for him more deeply than I'd originally supposed.'

'It doesn't matter. I'm moving on anyway.' Pru slapped her hand on the counter. 'You'd better go after Lew because Flynn might have fired him by now for kissing the bar staff. Or killed him and stuffed him under a boab tree. He was mad enough to do either.'

'Run it past me again, why did you and Lew kiss each other?' asked Rachel with renewed suspicion.

'Lew wanted to prove my feelings for Flynn were based on love and not lust.' She shook her head. 'Sounds daft but believe me, it made sense at the time.'

*   *   *

'Want cheering up, babe?' Toni asked Prudence later that evening as they worked in the kitchen, cooking up a storm for the customers.

Toni and Jimmy had come back relaxed and happy after their romantic afternoon together. Their obviously blossoming love for each other made

Pru feel worse. She didn't begrudge them, not one bit. In fact, she'd jokingly said to Jimmy if he wanted to make things legal between them, she'd love to have Toni as her step-mum.

But all their constant, lovey-dovey happiness was hard to take square on the chin when Pru was feeling so miserable in her heart.

For their sakes, she tried to keep the smile pinned on her face. Jimmy didn't suspect a thing, but she hadn't fooled Toni, not for a second.

'You look as though you could do with a good weep,' Toni said as she chucked a scoop of uncooked chips into the deep fryer, causing the fat to spit and sizzle.

'I'm not sad. I'm simply suffering from a bout of hay fever,' Prudence improvised.

Toni gave a snort. 'Think I was born yesterday? Come on, tell me what's been going on while Jimmy and I've been smooching out at the waterhole?'

'Nothing.' Pru had no intention of

giving Toni a blow-by-blow account of her stressful day.

'Babe, you are such a shocking liar.'

'Okay, let's just say I've had better days.'

'And you're feeling down?'

'Yes.'

'I've got news for you . . . I've got the very thing to make you feel better.'

'Stop there, Toni,' said Pru firmly, holding up both hands as if to ward off a blow. 'Don't suggest anything.'

'But . . . '

'No crazy hair colours, no tattoos, no piercings. I'm done with your methods of cheering up. They do not work!'

Toni laughed. 'I wasn't going to suggest any of those things.'

'You weren't?' Pru wasn't convinced. She was still suspicious.

'Of course not, babe.'

'What then?'

'How about we go bald?'

12

'Bald?' Prudence wasn't expecting that.

'Yep,' said Toni. 'We'll go bald. But not just for fun. We'll do it in aid of Cancer Research.' Her big grin was wider than the Grand Canyon.

'Yep. We'll shave off all our hair to raise money. It's an excellent cause. I know people who've had cancer. My auntie. My cousin. Several of my friends. So many people suffer from it. It's like an epidemic. I reckon anything we can do to find a cure is worthwhile. What do you say, babe?'

'Well . . . '

Okay, so Prudence wasn't keen on purple hair but if the alternative was no hair at all? That took some psychological adjustment. But, as Toni said, it was a worthwhile cause.

'We'll slap up posters all over Ibis Springs and tell everyone and anyone we can think of about it and ask them to sponsor us. I could even set up a blog about it.'

'Why can't we just dye our hair? Other people do that to raise money. It'd be much easier.' Pru really couldn't picture herself bald.

'But we've done the dyeing stuff for fun already. Let's go the extra distance.'

'I don't know about this, Toni. I'm leaving town in a couple of days. I don't fancy travelling through the outback looking like a bleached billiard ball.'

'I'll lend you a hat.'

'How thoughtful!' Pru dreaded to think what sort of hat she would think suitable. With Toni it could be anything from a woolly beanie to a biker's bandana. 'Anyway, there won't be time to organise the whole thing properly. I think we should give the idea a miss.'

'Don't be such a wuss. It'll be fun. You can stay on another week. It's no big deal and Jimmy will be pleased to have you around for a while longer. He's getting used to having a daughter around after all these years.'

'But I don't want to stay on longer.'

Toni grimaced. 'If this is about Flynn . . . '

'It's not!'

'So prove it. Stay.'

Prudence wished she hadn't been so quick to take up a challenge. Within half an hour, Toni had posters printed out from Jimmy's computer and plastered all over the bar with dollops of Blu Tack, and she had a nice stack of sponsor sheets ready to be filled in.

'We'll combine the head shaving with a karaoke night. It'll be a blast,' said Toni, who was now well into her stride.

'Oh my goodness,' said Pru. She was having more than second thoughts about the whole escapade.

'This is going to be the event of the year,' Toni carried on, her enthusiasm like rolling king wave. Prudence would just have to go along for the ride as gracefully as possible or be a big party pooper.

As the days whizzed by, Prudence

didn't hear a peep from Flynn. She missed him terribly but she'd eat dirt before repeating her request to have an affair with him — make that begging on her knees rather than requesting.

'We've a nice wodge of sponsorships,' said Toni, totting up the money pledges at the beginning of their big night. Jimmy's Place was already packed to bursting. Toni had excelled herself in rustling up support for the hair-shaving show.

'I'm not feeling very brave,' Pru admitted.

'Just shut your eyes and think of England,' grinned Toni.

'Better still, how about I just have a crew cut rather than a shave?'

'You can't renege now and let everyone down. They've paid good money to watch you being shorn. Look, they're all waiting.'

Prudence did look. There was a sea of expectant faces. Heck, she was committed to the eyeballs. There was only one thing for it: she screwed up her eyes as tight as they would go. 'Get on with it, then. Do your worst,' she instructed Toni through clenched teeth. 'But be gentle . . . '

* * *

Flynn entered the bar and did a double take. Pru was on karaoke centre stage and looking like some outer space alien in spangles and dangling parrot earrings. She was belting out a terrible rendition of *Sugar Baby Love* with an equally alien looking Toni. Her purple hair was a thing of the past. Both women's heads were now startling white domes.

'And that's it from the Baldettes,' yelled Toni at the end of the song. 'Thank you all for your support. Now who wants to take over the singing?'

Flynn elbowed his way through the noisy crowd and confronted Pru. 'What the hell have you done now?' he demanded with an abruptness bordering on rudeness.

'Are you going to sponsor me?' she said, her hands on her hips, her chin tipped in challenge mode.

'Sponsor you? What for? What is all this.' He flicked his hand towards her hairless head.

'I'm not doing this shearing stuff for fun you know. It's to raise money for cancer research.'

He shook his head in disbelief. 'And I thought you'd left town.'

'I was going to but Toni talked me into staying for a while longer so we could do this hair-shaving gig. But I'm leaving the day after tomorrow. It's all booked.' Pru held her breath and waited. What would he say? 'Stay, Prudence,' would be good. 'Let's have a final fling, Prudence,' would be even better. 'I love you, stay with me forever,' would be tops.

'Be happy,' he said after a moment's silence.

What?

'And take care.'

Be happy? Take care? *That was it?*

'And this is for the haircut.' Flynn stuffed some money into her hands, leaned over and gave her a brief kiss on the cheek before turning on his heel and leaving the bar. He didn't even give her the satisfaction of a backward glance.

Pru stood rooted to the spot, unaware of the couple of tears that slid down her cheeks and dripped off her jawbone. All that mattered was Flynn had gone. That he'd left. That it was finished.

The grand finale was over.

And her heart shattered.

★ ★ ★

'Why so down, kiddo? We did real good tonight,' said Toni as they served the last of the customers in the bar.

'Yes, we did.' Small comfort when her heart was broken beyond repair.

'So what's your problem now?'

'Nothing. Just feeling low after all the excitement, I guess,' she hedged, not wanting to share her misery with Toni. Just in case.

'You need cheering up, then.'

Pru shut her eyes and didn't deign to reply. She knew all about Toni's cheering up methods and they didn't work. Not one of them.

'What do you say about a camping trip to the lagoon?'

Pru's eyes snapped open. 'Flynn's lagoon?'

'The very one. Ibis Springs Lagoon. Famous for its birds and sunsets. It's considered the lovers' lane of the region. Tempted?'

'Hmm.' Pru was sorely tempted. She had wanted to see the lagoon ever since that first night when Flynn and Rachel had ridden off there for a picnic. She'd been told by locals it was a favourite watering hole and had heard glowing reports about its beauty, which had increased her desire to visit it for herself.

'So, you interested?' said Toni.

'Definitely, but what about this

place? Who's going to man the bar?'

'Jimmy can hold the fort on his own while you and I go. We'll camp out tomorrow night.'

'I'm leaving the next day. I should really spend my last night with Dad.'

'Let's go tonight, then. There's nothing to stop us.'

'But it's late.'

'So? Stop being so stuffy. Be adventurous for once. It won't take me long to get the camping stuff together. Jimmy will cope fine for the rest of the evening. All the hard work has already been done.'

It took them barely an hour to prepare their tent and provisions before the two women were rattling along the gravel track towards Flynn's boundary fence in Jimmy's rusty red truck. The headlights bobbed up and down and picked out scrubby bushes and rocks, throwing them into grotesque relief against the intense blackness.

The waning moon hadn't yet appeared but the stars spangled the vast expanse of dark velvet sky. It was a perfect night. Pru had never seen such unblemished starry skies until coming to Australia. The night sky back home was always infused with the tangerine glow of land-rooted streetlights.

It took them a while to reach the lagoon, which was fringed with ghost gums and paperbark trees. The air was punctured with frog song and the high-pitched drone of mosquitoes.

Using the headlights to illuminate their campsite, the women pitched the two-man tent. It was lucky Toni was an old hand at camping because Pru didn't have a clue which poles went where and made Toni laugh with her inept attempts. It wasn't long before Toni had a small campfire lit and the billycan boiling for a cup of cocoa.

'This is wonderful, Toni,' said Pru minutes later, blowing on the surface of her steaming tin cup. She inhaled deeply, savouring the combined scents of river mud, eucalyptus leaves, cocoa and the lavender oil they had slathered on their skin to repel the insects. 'Absolutely idyllic.'

'Yeah, it is. Jimmy's brought me out here a couple of times. I thought you'd appreciate it too.'

'Thanks, Toni. I do. I can't believe I might have left Ibis Springs and never visited it.'

'You wait until dawn. Hundreds of ibis will be here then, feeding on the river flats. That's why the early settlers called the area Ibis Springs. We'll turn in soon so we can be up with the sun and see all the birds.'

★　★　★

Flynn drove straight home. He couldn't bear to stay at Jimmy's Place and watch Pru. He desperately wanted to ask her to stay on at Ibis Springs, but he didn't know if he could override a lifetime of self-imposed independence and plead with her to remain. And, more importantly, he didn't know how she'd react. He had to face it, he was scared to take the gamble she might turn him down. He was a sore loser at the best of times but now his heart, his very soul, was at risk.

Sleep escaped him so he attempted to immerse himself in paperwork. He wanted to lose himself completely in columns of figures so he could forget Amaryllis. He had to get his head straight again. She tied him so tightly in knots he didn't know where he was or what he was doing any more.

And she was leaving town.

But he knew it was for the best. He simply had to wait it out until she was on that darn bus and off to wherever she was going to blitz next. Maybe then he could get his life back on track.

Just maybe.

He smacked the desk with his fist, making the papers jump. Who was he kidding? His life would never be the same again. Prudence Stark had derailed him good and proper. There was no going back.

He was no longer content to

squander his life on the fortunes of Ibis Springs Station. There was no point to it anymore. Without Pru, it was an empty vessel, a waste of time and energy.

Pru, with her intense love affair with life, had made him realise what a half-baked existence he'd been living. A non-life devoid of love and warmth, with no firm prize at the end but an empty house where there should be children, an empty bed where there should be his wife.

Perhaps that's what his father had been seeking in all those failed relationships: a soul mate to share his heart.

The realisation was like a sharp pain. Suddenly Flynn didn't blame him anymore. His dad had taken the risks on love, and lost. But it had been his choice and one he'd made over and over again with no apparent long-lasting regrets. Maybe Flynn should learn from him rather than trying to avoid making mistakes. Take the gamble for once, just as he did in business, without a qualm.

It was a terrifying yet exhilarating thought, gambling on love.

Flynn tossed his pen down on to the pile of papers on his desk and massaged his skull. Tension was his best buddy these days. It never left him.

Only one thing could appease it.

Or should he say, only one girl.

So perhaps it was finally time for Flynn Maguire to grow up and start living? Yes! It was! Tomorrow he'd go and see Pru at the very earliest opportunity and beg her, on bended knees if necessary, to stay . . .

It was very late when the phone rang. Flynn had been on the edge of sleep. He scowled at the stridently ringing phone and turned his back on it, burying his head under the pillow. But the phone kept ringing. It cut off. Flynn relaxed. But then it began ringing again. Finally he snatched up the receiver and barked a curt 'yes'.

'Is that you, Flynn?' Jimmy said.

'What do you want, Jimmy?'

'Sorry if I woke you.'

'You did,' he said with sleep-induced bluntness.

'But it's important.'

'Go on, then.' Flynn rubbed his hand over his eyes and back of his neck to dispel his grogginess.

'One of your jackaroos just mentioned there's been a big croc sighted at the lagoon.'

'Yeah, that's right.' Flynn yawned. 'We've warned everyone to keep an eye out until we can catch the brute and move him to a safer location.'

Jimmy swore.

'What's the problem, mate?' said Flynn, instantly alert at Jimmy's change of tone.

'The girls have gone to camp there tonight. They don't know anything about it. The lad's only just told me about the croc.'

'Girls?' In his gut, Flynn already knew the answer.

'Prudence and Toni. They left a couple of hours ago. They won't stand a chance if that croc crosses their path. I can't get out there quickly enough, the girls took my truck. I'm going to need to borrow someone's'

Flynn was already half way out of the bed and reaching for his jeans. 'Get there as fast as you can. I'm on my way. Bring back up.' He abruptly disconnected the phone and wasted few seconds snatching up a rifle and bullets and heading for the utility. There was probably nothing to worry about, but Flynn wasn't taking any chances. Not with his exotic flower girl at risk.

13

Pru was finding it hard to sleep. Put her next to a busy city junction and she'd have no bother. Try a ghetto blaster pumping out rap two inches from her ear, again no sweat. But a cacophony of frogs was driving her loopy. It didn't help that Toni snored like a gorilla with enlarged adenoids, and mosquitoes were whining a whisper away from her face, preparing to swoop down for a blood-sucking feast. She was going to look like a terminal case of measles by the end of this camping jaunt. A great addition to her bald head and tattooed bottom.

It didn't help that the ground was as hard as lead. She was convinced every little rock and stick had magnetised to the down side of her sleeping bag. However she wriggled and jiggled, she couldn't get comfortable. Camping sucked.

How long until dawn? It was anyone's guess.

She tried to do the *Sound of Music* trick of thinking of all her favourite things, but she wasn't as successful as Maria. The only favourite thing she could think of was Flynn Maguire and she didn't want to go there because thinking of Flynn only made her want to bawl her eyes out.

She scrunched her eyes shut and decided to count her breaths. She was up to goodness knows how many, and getting drowsy in spite of her discomfort, when something big and heavy slammed against the tent.

She shot upright and stared at the canvas. She couldn't make out anything in the dark. What in goodness' name had it been? A rogue steer? A kangaroo? Neither of which she'd like to meet face-to-face by torchlight.

What-ever-it-was bashed the tent again. Pru trembled. A flimsy wall of canvas was no security blanket. She was dead scared.

What if it was a dingo? Did they get dingoes here? Dingoes had sharp teeth. They could bite. They could hurt.

Or perhaps it was a psychopath. Did they have those in the middle of Australian Outback Nowhere? She hoped not. She didn't want to meet an axe-wielding maniac while clad in nothing but a pair of briefs and a tank top.

Actually, she didn't want to meet an axe-wielding maniac, period.

'Toni,' Pru grabbed her friend's shoulder and gave her a rough shake. 'Wake up. Something's trying to get inside the tent.'

Toni rolled over and cuddled back down. 'It's nothing,' she mumbled. 'Go to sleep. Quit being a worry wart.'

'It *is* something!' hissed Pru. 'And it's big.'

Whatever it was hit the tent again, making the whole structure shake. This time Toni gave it a cursory glance.

'Probably one of the boys from town messing about — TRYING TO SCARE

US,' she said in a loud voice and then snuggled down again with a sleepy giggle.

'Well, he's succeeding,' said Pru through gritted teeth. 'GO AWAY, WHOEVER YOU ARE, OR I'LL CALL THE COPS!'

Her yelled empty threat didn't work. The tent pitched and juddered a couple more times. The next moment the canvas was ripped apart and a big, black, bulky creature lunged in towards the women.

Pru screamed and jack-knifed her legs tight to her chest, her heart pounding in horror. The beam of light from her small torch revealed a huge saltwater crocodile. It zeroed in on Toni. Toni, groggy with sleep, wasn't as quick as Prudence in moving out of the way. The crocodile sank its teeth into her sleeping bag, taking her legs in his massive jaws and began yanking her out of the tent.

Pru screamed again and dived for Toni who was too shocked to do anything to help herself. The torch went flying as Pru tugged and tugged, but the crocodile was no match for Pru. It pulled both women from the tent and into the night. Pru guessed it was dragging them towards the lagoon but it was hard to tell which direction they were heading in the dark, especially in her confused and panicked state.

All she knew was she had to do something fast or they were lost. Pru let go of Toni's arm and sprang on to the crocodile's back, beating it with her bare fists, trying to find its eyes to gouge and maim. Oh for a weapon. Her fingers were nothing more than whispers against the hard studded surface of the reptile.

Without warning, the saltwater monster suddenly released Toni's legs and turned on Pru, knocking her sideways, its massive jaws snapping and slashing at her. It bit into her arm and began pulling her towards the water. The pain was excruciating. Pru tried to yank her arm free but the creature had locked on to her like a police wheel-clamp on an illegally parked car.

She flailed with her other arm and hit the leathery snout of the animal. She thrust her fingers into what she hoped, in her panic, were its eyes, but they turned out to be its nostril cavities. The crocodile shook her hard and she flipped back and forth like a beanbag doll.

Pru valiantly tried to stall their treacherous journey towards the water. She wouldn't stand a hope in hell if the crocodile got her into the lagoon. He'd drown her for sure. In desperation, she tried to dig her heels into the dirt but her bare feet slithered over the slippery, smooth surface, finding no purchase against the hard, sun-baked mud.

Oh God, Oh God, she prayed, save me, please . . .

They hit the lagoon.

Whoosh! The cold, brackish water shocked her. Pru gasped. Big mistake. Her mouth and nose filled with the rank water. She thrashed about, spitting and gagging, but the big crocodile went into a series of tight death rolls.

It was like being in a huge washing machine. Pru was belted from side to side, becoming totally disorientated. I've had it, she thought in despair. I'm going to die.

Suddenly they broke the surface. Pru frantically sucked in a lungful of air before the creature pulled her back under water to continue its deadly rolling routine.

Pru could no longer feel pain, only numb panic. She tried to keep from sobbing because then she'd lose what little breath she had.

They broke the surface again and she gasped for more glorious, life-giving air. The crocodile loosened its hold and Pru took advantage, pushing against the lagoon's muddy bottom. She reached out with her good arm for a low branch of a dead tree, which was thrusting from the water close by to her.

She missed.

The crocodile lunged for her again. Jaws of spiked, razor-sharp teeth closed around her leg. It jerked her hard under the water and rolled and rolled and rolled . . .

For whatever reason, the reptile relaxed its hold again. Pru struggled to find purchase under her feet. She felt a rock. Hallelujah! She kicked away from it, wrenching herself upwards with all her might, breaking through the water's surface. She made a wild grab for the tree again and this time succeeded in snagging a branch. She held onto the branch with all her might. Desperation lent her a previously unsuspected reserve of strength, and she hauled herself up, the water cascading from her body.

She clutched at the branch and tried to wriggle further up the tree but her savaged arm hampered progress.

In the dark, all she could make out below were a pair of yellow eyes and a hideous shape.

Pru whimpered and scrabbled higher up the dead tree. The jaws gnashed just below her foot. In terror she lost her footing, slipping down the smooth grey trunk of the bleached gum. The crocodile clamped its teeth over her lower leg. Pru howled in pain and despair.

She was going to die . . .

There was a loud, sharp crack.

Then another.

Unbelievably, the creature loosened its jaws and fell writhing into the black water beneath Pru. There was a third crack. Pru hugged the tree and began to cry hysterically.

Relief washed through her in giant waves. Someone had come to save her.

★   ★   ★

'Pru? Toni?'

Flynn could hear the gut-wrenching sobs. He spun his spotlight across the water where it slashed the darkness like a laser, illuminating the lagoon. Its beam fell on the pale, shivering body panic-welded to the tree.

Pru! She was alive!

'Stay there, honey. I'm coming for you!' What a damn fool thing to say! That blood-streaked, traumatised woman wasn't going anywhere fast, but he'd had to say something to let her know he was there and ready to help her. Flynn slung the leather-strapped rifle over his shoulder and waded up to his waist into the lagoon.

'You can let go, sweetheart. I've got you,' he said when he reached out for her. One hand clamped around her waist, his other raised up to prise her from the tree.

'C-C-Can't,' she said in a cruelly hoarse whisper. The earlier wild scream-ing had lacerated her throat.

'Yes, you can, Pru. Take it nice and gently. I'm here. I'll catch you. You're safe now.'

'The croc?'

'Dead.'

'Any more?'

'I certainly hope not! But I don't intend to hang around to find out. Let's go, hon. And now.' He didn't want to take any more risks than necessary.

Pru began to ease her death-grip on the branch and then all strength drained away and she fell against Flynn. His arms wrapped around her tightly and he hugged her close before wading carefully back to the bank, keeping out a watchful eye for any other crocodiles. By the time he'd reached the land, Jimmy had arrived with a couple of other men. They'd left their ute lights blazing to illuminate the bank.

Pru was handed over to Jimmy while the others hauled Flynn out of the stinking, sucking mud.

'Radio the Flying Doctor,' commanded Flynn. 'She's lost a lot of blood.'

'Where's Toni?' Jimmy asked as he laid Pru on the ground.

Pru, dazed and shivering, pointed to the campsite. It looked as if a hurricane had blown through it. The tent was a crumpled mess. Pots and pans were strewn around. One of the sleeping bags was tossed to one side.

But there was no sign of Toni.

'I'll deal with Pru. You go and search for her,' said Flynn. He efficiently began checking Pru's wounds with his large, gentle hands. He ripped off his shirt and tore it into strips, bandaging her savaged arm and then leg, while the others ran over to the camping ground.

'She's here,' yelled Jimmy. 'In the truck.'

'Okay?' whispered Pru. She was shaking with post-traumatic shock and finding it hard to speak coherently.

'She's fine,' reassured Flynn even though he had no idea. 'Don't worry. You're both safe now.'

He wrapped her in his arms again and rocked her trembling body. 'You're safe,' he murmured again and kissed the smooth top of her shaven head.

★   ★   ★

Pru woke up in a bright, white room filled with stainless steel and tubes. Most of the tubes seemed to be poking into her body. There were beeps and whirrs of equipment. In the background she could hear muted voices. Her whole body was absorbed with incredible pain. She couldn't move, couldn't speak.

A nightmare.

She tried to rail against the pain, the intrusive tubes and antiseptic smell until there was a sharp sting in her arm. And then the intense throbbing went away and she was floating . . . floating . . . floating . . .

When she awoke again, someone was holding her hand. It felt good. Comforting and warm. Reassuring and stable. Right.

She cracked open an eye to see to whose hand it was. Ah Flynn. And he was as golden and gorgeous as ever, if a little rumpled and worn around the edges. He was wearing a blue checked shirt and jeans that looked as though they'd been slept in for at least a year. His hair was tangled, as if he'd been repeatedly running his fingers through it. Golden stubble haloed his chin.

A dreamy warm glow infused her. Flynn was by her side, holding her hand as if it were an anchor, and his mussed state meant the Mighty Flynn was feeling mighty vulnerable. Perhaps because of her . . . ?

It took her a few moments to register, in her hazy, drugged state, that while she was blatantly staring — and probably grinning — at him, he was doing exactly the same to her.

The realisation unsettled her. Made her shy.

'What? Do I have a smudge on my nose or something?' she murmured to hide her sudden confusion, sucking in her soppy smile, trying to scowl. Her throat was still sore and hoarse from all the screaming and swallowing of dirty lagoon water. It wasn't even a sexy hoarse, but more like half-strangled chicken. Just her luck!

A smile lit Flynn's eyes. 'Trust you to wake after hours of unconsciousness and come out with a smart-assed crack,' he said, his voice soft and warm.

'Well, you were giving me the heebie-jeebies staring at me like that. Where am I?' She gave an eye-roll around the room.

'Hospital.'

'You don't say,' she rasped. 'I think I had managed to work that out. But where precisely? It looks a bit fancy for Ibis Springs. Unless Joannie has done a makeover.'

'You're in Darwin.'

'Darwin?' It came out as a raw squeak. 'That's miles away. How come?'

'The Royal Flying Doctor brought you here after the attack. You were in a pretty bad state, sweetheart. You'd lost a lot of blood.'

She shivered and lay there for a moment. She summoned her courage and dared to ask, 'What about Toni? Is she okay?'

'She's fine. She's here too. Jimmy's with her.'

'What'd happened to her? Where'd you find her?'

'After the croc made off with you, she managed to crawl to the truck and lock herself in the cab. She's suffered a few puncture wounds to her legs and loss of blood, but she's recovering well. Thanks to you.'

Pru glanced at her own bandaged arms and legs.

'You didn't get off quite so lightly. That's what happens when you're a hero.' His face tightened, his eyes glittering with a dangerous light. 'Dammit, Pru, you could have been killed pulling a stunt like that. No-one in their right mind would try wrestling a croc.'

'I couldn't have sat back and watched Toni be dragged into the water for a croc snack!' Tears filled her eyes, her chest heaved with latent, pent up emotion.

'I know, honey, I know. I guess I'd have done the same.' He did that hair-ruffling thing and grimaced in a self-deprecating way. 'But you know, Amaryllis, you had me really scared last night. I thought I'd lost you. When I came across the campsite and saw it trashed, I was so scared. I'd hate to think what would have happened if I'd been any later. That Big Daddy was ready to pull you back down into the water.'

Pru shut her eyes, shuddering as the horrifying attack replayed itself in her mind.

Flynn squeezed her hand and said in a voice almost as hoarse as hers, 'I don't think I can survive many more nights like that. Promise me you'll do no more madcap heroics.'

'No immediate plans to,' said Pru, still with her eyes tightly closed. A tear leaked out from under one eyelid as she contemplated how close she had been to death.

'Hey, sweetheart.'

Pru sniffled and Flynn grabbed a tissue from the bedside cabinet and awkwardly dabbed at her tears.

'Cry all you want, babe.'

'Don't think I can stop anyway.' She

gave a watery half-smile as her tears began in earnest. She tried to raise her hand to her face to swipe at the tears and try and block out the memories, but the bandages restricted her movement. And anyway, it hurt too much to move them.

'You'll be back on your feet and out of here in no time,' said Flynn trying to be upbeat.

'Yeah, I know.' A sob bubbled up and spilled over. 'Sorry,' she said again.

'Don't be,' he said.

At that moment one of the nurses knocked on the door and came in. 'What's going on here?' she said bustling up to the bed. 'Feeling a bit emotional, are we? It's to be expected. Perhaps your fiancé should leave you to sleep for a while?' She gave Flynn another hard stare.

'Fiancé?' Pru cried harder.

'Sweetheart . . . '

'I think it's best you leave,' said the nurse propelling Flynn through the door with no-nonsense bluntness. 'You can come back and visit your sweetheart later, when she's feeling better. She needs plenty of rest to speed her recovery or she'll remain in hospital a lot longer.' She closed the door on him with a decided click.

'Men!' she said to Prudence with a short laugh. 'Don't you just love 'em! But you have to be tough with them, too. They're just kids at heart and need plenty of guidance. You remember that when you two tie the knot. Now, there's no need to get so upset, luvvy . . . '

* * *

Flynn lent against the wall outside of Pru's private room. He shut his eyes and pinched the bridge of his nose. He sighed. He'd have to come clean soon and confess to the staff he wasn't Pru's fiancé. He'd initially said he was so he could have unlimited access to her bedside. Because that was exactly where he wanted to be. Needed to be. How he yearned to gather her up and hug her close. He hated seeing her so vulnerable and small lying there in the big white hospital bed with all those tubes and machines attached to her. He wanted to hold and protect her . . . forever.

Forever!

Yes, that summed it up perfectly. As soon as Prudence was well enough, he'd ask her to marry him and live at Ibis Springs forever. Or for however long she wanted. He would take whatever he could get and blow the station. He needed her, wanted her so much more than the patch of land that had obsessed him most of his adult life. It was a liberating feeling, finally realising loving Prudence was all that mattered.

Joy bubbled within him, making him ridiculously light-headed. He shook his head to clear it.

'You okay, mate?' It was the doctor, on his way to another patient.

'Yeah, never better. Though I hate seeing Pru in such pain.'

'Don't worry about her. She's going

to be fine. We've pumped her full of antibiotics and we'll be monitoring her progress carefully over the next few hours. With luck, she should be ready to go home in a few days.' He clapped him on the back and moved on down the corridor.

'By the way, loved the tatt,' he threw over his shoulder. 'Very cute. Very sexy. Must ask my wife to have one done.'

'Tatt?'

'The tattoo.' He chuckled. 'I saw it when giving her a needle.'

Flynn frowningly watched the doctor disappear into another room. What tattoo? Prudence wasn't the sort to have tattoos.

Or was she?

He thought about her outrageous clothes, her dyed hair, her shaven head. Hmm. A tattoo wasn't so beyond the pale, then.

His curiosity was piqued. He'd have to ask Pru about it, when she was feeling stronger.

In the meantime, Flynn decided to

find the cafeteria and buy himself a coffee. He'd only gone a couple of steps when a young woman accosted him. She was small and pale with a pile of red hair on top of her pretty head, secured with artful messiness. She was wearing neat white shorts and an emerald green top. There were a lot of gold chains around her neck and wrists.

'Excuse me,' she said. Her voice was straight from the Mother country: cool, clipped and classy.

She sounded just like Pru.

'Yes, ma'am?'

'I'm looking for Prudence Stark. Is this her room?' She waved a hand towards the closed door of Pru's private ward.

'Yes, and you are?'

The woman blinked. 'Who wants to know?'

Flynn held out his hand. 'Flynn Maguire. I'm . . . er . . . her fiancé.'

The woman blinked again, more rapidly this time. She sucked in a short breath and the expelled it with a dainty whistle.

'Fiancé? Pru's engaged? No! I don't believe it. She's only been away a few weeks. She'd never work that fast. Unless . . . Oh Lord, she's probably done it to get back at . . . ' She tailed off and then subjected Flynn to a swift up and down. She raised her dainty brows and said, 'I think I'd better introduce myself. I'm Katrina, Prudence's sister.'

'Sister?' Flynn hadn't known she had one. Pru hadn't talked at all about her personal life in England. It was as if nothing else existed between them but the here and now at Ibis Springs.

'Well, step-sister to be exact. How is she? I was told she was attacked by a crocodile. Is that right?'

'Yes. How did you find out?'

'I turned up at her dad's for a surprise visit and they told me she was here. I've never been so shocked. A crocodile for goodness' sake!'

She gave Flynn another swift once

over. 'So you're her fiancé. Well, well. I still find that hard to believe. Nothing against you, of course. Don't be offended.'

'No offence taken,' said Flynn in a bemused way.

'I must see her. Find out what's been going on.' She gave Flynn another assessing look, which spoke volumes. 'And pump her for information that's been sadly lacking in her brief phone calls.'

'She's in here.' Flynn indicated the door of the private room. 'But she's still fragile. Don't give her too much of a hard time.'

'As if.'

He gave her a wary look and then tapped on Pru's door, poking his head around it. The nurse was packing away the blood pressure unit, preparing to leave.

Prudence had stopped crying, but the way she was staring at him he reckoned it wouldn't take much to start her off again.

'Prudence, you have a visitor,' he said and held open the door wide.

Pru's jaw dropped as she saw Katrina. Katrina looked equally stunned.

'Pru?' she said, horrified. 'My goodness.' And she rushed over to Pru's bedside. 'You look terrible, darling, and what's happened to your lovely hair . . . Did they have to shave it off?'

Pru gave a twisted smile. 'No, no. I did that on purpose. For charity.'

'Oh my.' Kat clapped a hand over her mouth.

'But it was purple before that, sis.'

'Pru! You didn't!'

'And pink before that,' she said, her tone now smug as she watched her sister's reaction.

'Oh Pru!' Kat smacked her hands gleefully.

'And before that, blonde.'

'You actually went and did it! I honestly thought you'd never dye your hair.'

'I said I would.'

'Yes, but to actually do it . . . '

'Oh ye of little faith.'

'And the slinky underwear? Did you go for that too?'

Pru shot a glance at Flynn, whose eyebrows had risen much more than a fraction, before focussing back on Kat. Well, in the scheme of things, there was no point denying it. Flynn knew too much about her.

'Yup.'

'And you got engaged too, you rascal!'

Pru switched her attention back to Flynn, who was now looking sheepish. 'Ah, well, about that . . . ' she said.

'Because of Dean?'

'Who's Dean?' said Flynn trying to keep up with their rapid conversation.

'No, not because of Dean,' said Pru starkly.

'He'll be so wild you've replaced him so quickly. So is this the guy you said you were going to pick up?' Kat laughed delightedly.

'I'm missing something here,' said Flynn. 'Who is Dean? And for the record, I did the picking up.'

But the girls weren't listening to him. They'd moved on.

'So how come you got attacked by a crocodile?' demanded Kat.

'She did the attacking and it was in a lagoon,' said Flynn. 'And I still want to know who Dean is.'

'But Pru would never fight a crocodile!' exclaimed Kat, wide-eyed. 'She's too timid.'

'Much you know about Pru,' said Flynn. 'She'd take on the world if she thought it was the right thing to do.'

'Golly, sis, you must have had a radical change these past few weeks,' said Kat with a big grin. 'Take my hat off to you, girl, I didn't think you'd rise to the challenge. Wait until Dean finds out you're engaged. He'll be so mad. He wants you to come home and take up where you left off.'

'I'm not engaged. Flynn's not my fiancé,' said Pru bluntly. 'He lied. And why does Dean want me home? What about Fab-Abs Gail?'

'But he told me he was your fiancé!' Kat turned accusing eyes on Flynn, her playfulness dissipating swiftly.

'He's apparently told everyone he is, but he's most definitely not.' Pru glared at him too. 'Now tell me about Dean and Gail.'

'Well, that's gratitude after saving you from that old salt,' Flynn said with a lightness he was far from feeling and wondering who the hell this Dean was and why the bloke wanted Pru home.

'Dean is just someone from home,' said Prudence darkly. 'And as for you, Flynn Maguire, you can't say goodbye and good riddance to me one minute and then say we're engaged to be married the next. It doesn't make sense. Hot one minute, cold the next. I'm confused.'

'I did not say 'good riddance!'' Flynn defended himself. 'And I'm confused too. Who is this Dean? Someone special?'

'You gave me the brush off, admit it! And as for Dean, he's my ex-fiancé.'

'I thought saying goodbye was for the best, but I've changed my mind. We have too much unfinished business between us,' he said with stout tolerance. 'And I didn't know you'd been engaged.'

'I can't think of any business between us, and my being engaged has nothing to do with you.'

Kat butted in. 'Dean jilted her just before the wedding, the rat. Which is why she went to Bali. It was meant to be her honeymoon.'

'Oh Lord,' said Flynn. 'Was that why you were hitting the cocktails?'

'You got drunk?' said Kat, amazed. 'But you never drink.'

'She did that night and passed out on me,' said Flynn with feeling.

'Prudence! Oh my.'

'And while we're sharing information, how about you tell me about your tattoo?' said Flynn. 'Talking about any other business and all.'

Pru's cheeks glowed red and rosy in an instant. 'How did you know about that?'

'The doctor told me.'

'What tattoo?' said Katrina. 'Surely you haven't had a tattoo done too? You hate needles!'

'Grief,' said Pru, scrunching tight her eyes. 'Nothing's sacred. I thought there was a code of ethics or something to protect patients' personal records?'

'You're my fiancée so it doesn't count. So what does it say, this tattoo of yours?'

'I am not your fiancée, so it does count. And you don't know what it says? What a pity,' she said sarcastically. 'I'm surprised the doc didn't tell you.'

'I wish he had. Come on, what does it say, Prudence?'

'Yes, what does it say?' asked Katrina, intrigued.

'I'm not telling.' Pru clamped her lips together. 'It's private.'

Flynn regarded her steadily. 'As I said, Amaryllis, we have unfinished business . . . I'll leave you two ladies to catch up on family things. I'll be seeing you.'

14

Flynn drove the hire car into the hospital parking area. He'd been to Ibis Springs for a few days catching up on jobs. There was also a cyclone alert for the North-West, which meant he'd had to batten down the hatches at the station to minimise damage, as well as buy in extra supplies. Kat had stayed in Darwin with Prudence but had now returned to England. It was time to collect Prudence, fly her back to Ibis Springs and beat the cyclone.

Prudence didn't know it yet, but she was going to spend the next few days recuperating at his place. She thought she was going to Jimmy's when discharged from the hospital, but Flynn had cleared it with the older man that Flynn would take her back to Ibis Springs Station and care for her until she was fit. Jimmy had been fine about it. As it was, he had his work cut out caring for Toni as well as running the bar. He didn't need another patient.

Flynn locked the car and took long, measured strides towards the hospital's main entrance. He spotted Pru before she saw him. She was in the reception area sitting on a hard-backed chair and flicking through an out-of-date woman's magazine. Her hair had grown back slightly, so that it was a soft brown fuzz over her scalp. It gave her a sweet, elfin look. She was wearing her pink muslin shirt with a pair of snug denim shorts. Her face was devoid of make-up. Apart from her wounded arms and legs, that were a network of stitches and dressings, she looked much more like the brunette Bali babe of his initial acquaintance than the psychedelic Debbie Harry barmaid of the last few weeks.

'Amaryllis,' said Flynn. 'You ready to go?'

She gave a start, tossing the magazine back on to the pile of dog-eared back issues. 'Where's Dad? I thought he was collecting me.'

'He's busy at the bar. I'm taking you home. The weather's blowing up and we've got to get back to Ibis Springs before trouble hits.'

'What sort of trouble?'

'There's a cyclone off the coast and heading this way.'

'Is it dangerous?'

'Not if we take precautions, and that means moving fast. I don't want to be grounded in Darwin.'

'Let's get going then.'

'As Flynn drove them towards the airport, Pru said conversationally, 'You know, I really didn't think I'd see you again.'

'Because of Dean? It'd take more than an old boyfriend to scare me off.'

'He was my fiancé, not just a boyfriend.'

'He's past history. A big ex. Nothing to do with us now.' He put emphasis on the 'us', just to let her know he meant business.

'Didn't it worry you that he wanted me to go home with Kat?'

'If the bloke loved you, he'd be here now, taking you back himself, not letting your kid step-sister play courier.'

'He has work commitments.'

'He's a loser.'

'I could give it another go. It's what he wants, since things didn't work out with Gail.'

'Is that what you want? Really? Be honest now, Prudence.'

Pru stared out the window. 'No,' she sighed. 'I've moved on. I'm a different person. I've changed.'

'Good. So why are we discussing Dean?'

'I just thought you should know that I did think about it seriously. Dean was part of my life — my dreams — for a very long time.'

'Amaryllis, that bloke had his chance. Now it's mine. You with me or not? Your call.'

She stared at him. 'Yes. I'm with you, Maguire.'

'You sure of that?'

She shrugged. 'As sure as I'll ever be.'

'Good.'

'Is that so?'

'Yep. Now how about you tell me about that tattoo which so took the doctor's fancy.'

'Ah.'

'I've been imagining all sorts of designs. You'd be surprised.'

'Don't let your imagination runaway with you. It's a very small, unobtrusive tattoo. If ever you saw it, which you probably won't, you'd be very disappointed.'

'Let me be the judge of that.'

Pru snorted, then fell silent for the rest of the ride to the airport.

Once they were airborne, it didn't take Pru long to realise they weren't flying back to the township of Ibis Springs but to Flynn's station.

'I think I'm being kidnapped,' she murmured as she gazed out of the light aircraft's window and regarded the wide expanse of red cattle country.

'Define kidnapped.'

'Being taken somewhere against your will.'

'Can you honestly say you mind?' asked Flynn. 'It's just that Jimmy's really busy caring for Toni as well as the bar and I thought I could do my bit . . . And I did ask you if you were with me or not . . . '

Prudence was aware, for all his confident manner, Flynn was holding his breath, anxious for her reply.

So did she? Did she really, really mind Flynn was whisking her away to his home rather than Jimmy's?

Excitement suddenly flared in the pit of her stomach. Deep in her heart she knew the answer.

'Will it be just the two of us or will Lew be there?' she said, deciding to play for time.

'Lew's over with Rachel. Her manager resigned the other day and so Lew's been helping her out.'

'How are things between them?'

'Pretty steamy, thanks to you. I

reckon it won't be long before I'll be looking for another station manager. I think wedding bells are in the air.' He gave her a brief glance, his lips twisted in a slight smile, his eyes warm and watchful. 'You've turned out a bit of a matchmaker, what with Jimmy and Toni, and Lew and Rachel.' He paused and then added, 'How are you doing with us, kid?'

'I wasn't aware we were in the equation.' She sounded calm and matter-of-fact, but her heart was skittering in her chest like a captured bird at his loaded question.

'Does that mean you want me to turn around the plane and take you back to Jimmy's?'

Startled by the rawness of his question, she shot him a sideways glance, 'Would you do that for me if I asked?'

'If that's what you truly wanted.' His smile was grim and she could hear the disappointment in his voice above the noise of the Cessna's engine. 'Just say the word, Pru, and I'll take you to Jimmy's.'

Pru sucked on her lower lip. All their playfulness had gone. Crunch time loomed. Could she do it? Did she want to?

'Pru? I need your decision now. The clouds are banking up. We don't have much time. This is your last chance. We turn back now or keep going ahead.'

And she knew he wasn't just talking of the plane ride.

She took a deep, long breath. 'Keep going,' she said with a confidence she was far from feeling.

A muscle worked in his cheek. There was a split second silence. Flynn wasn't stupid. They both knew this would lead to a dangerous shift in their relationship.

'Are you sure?' he said finally.

'Yes.' She gave a nervous laugh. 'Are you?'

Flynn reached over and grabbed her hand. He squeezed it hard and reassuringly. 'Yes. Very.'

The plane suddenly hit turbulence. 'Hold tight. The flying is going to get a little rough. Bags are in the pocket by the door if you need them.'

Pru smiled to herself. Romantic it wasn't, but very necessary. Flynn really knew how to show a girl a good time. She took out a bag just in case.

They didn't speak again as Flynn had to concentrate on piloting the plane, holding the aircraft against the strong, buffeting winds. But in a while, Flynn brought the small aircraft down on to the makeshift airstrip and taxied it into the hangar. The wind was roaring, the clouds streaking across the sky in a solid bank of grey heralding the onslaught of the storm.

'Let's move,' he said, grabbing Pru's elbow and steering her towards the utility truck parked nearby. The temperature had plummeted. Fat drops of rain hit the dirt and bounced on the dust around them.

They slammed the ute's doors shut and Flynn revved the engine. 'It might be a hairy ride home. Make sure you're belted in properly. Here goes . . . '

Within seconds the dust had turned to mud. It was like driving through a river of melted chocolate. The ute slewed first this way and then that. Pru marvelled at Flynn's skill as he kept the vehicle from bogging in the deep ruts that now grooved the dirt road, or from being swept along by the racing water currents. The window-wipers worked hard against the torrential rain but it was still nigh on impossible to see where they were driving.

Pru tensed, trying to watch the road, then decided it was better to keep her eyes shut. If she didn't, she was in danger of cracking all her teeth because she was clenching her jaw so tightly.

Thunder roared, lighting cracked. Pru clung to the dashboard to stop herself from being jolted around, her injuries screaming from the buffeting. She sent up endless prayers they'd be delivered safely.

'Not long now, sweetheart,' shouted

Flynn over the clamour of the storm. 'Only a few hundred metres.'

How could he tell? Pru cracked open an eye. She could see nothing but water and mud. She was glad Flynn knew what he was doing and where they were heading.

And then the ute hit something hard and stopped dead in its tracks. Flynn and Pru were almost garrotted by the seatbelts.

'Dammit!' Flynn hit the wheel with the flat of his hand. 'Are you okay?'

'Fine. Just shaken.' Along with a good dose of whiplash and burst stitches, but she didn't want to sound like a wuss. They were in enough trouble without adding to it with her aches and pains.

'Damn, but we're so close.'

'We can make it on foot,' said Pru trying to sound upbeat, but horribly aware of how the rain was lashing down and the wind screeching.

'No we can't. Not with you just out of hospital.'

'Wasn't it you who said I was tough?'

'Not that tough.' He smiled and stroked the side of her cheek with his fore finger. 'We'll sit tight for a while. You never know, it might blow itself out.'

'Does it usually?'

Flynn sighed and slung his arm around her shoulders. 'No.'

'So let's make a dash for it now.'

'We'd be too vulnerable out there.' He flicked his hand at the storm.

'And we're not here?'

'I don't want to alarm you, Amaryllis, but it's the lesser of the two evils.'

'I see. So we sit here and do what? Play I-Spy or sing *A Thousand Green Bottles Hanging on the Wall*?'

'As there's not too much to see and I've heard your singing, how about we get to know each other better?'

'Okay. But I warn you, I am very boring.'

'That's a matter of opinion.'

'It's true.'

'Well, to avoid disappointment, perhaps I'll just kiss you instead.' His arm across her shoulder tightened and he began to lower his head.

'Oh, really!' she giggled as she felt her pulses rocket and blood steam at the mere thought of kissing Flynn again.

'Yes, really. Kiss me, Prudence ... ' He leaned closer and was just drawing her into the sweetest, dreamiest of kisses when the ute shifted.

'Goodness,' squeaked Pru. 'I've heard about the ground moving ... '

Flynn raised his head. There was a sudden deep, worried crease between his eyes. The ute shifted again, as if it was on a huge sheet of ice.

'Great. We're moving.'

'And that's not good?'

'Being swept away could be the end of us. We'd best get out.'

The ute slid sideways and began to slowly rotate. 'We'll have to get out your side.' Flynn leant over and shoved open the door and propelled Pru out at the same time.

She gasped and staggered as she hit the icy water. The driving rain slashed at her face. She was knee-deep in red muddy water. The road had morphed into a shallow, gushing river. Flynn jumped out the ute next to Pru and roughly grabbed her elbow, hauling her through the streaming water. It tugged at their legs, trying to pull them in its relentless, broiling wake. It took vital minutes before they managed to reach the side of the road.

'Hold on to my waist. I'll try and protect you from the worst of the rain,' yelled Flynn. 'We haven't far to go.'

It wasn't far but it took forever to reach the homestead. Several times they slipped and fell headlong into the liquid mud and expended precious energy trying to get back on their feet. Pru was exhausted but tried to push past the fatigue barrier. All her limbs ached. Some of her cuts had reopened and were bleeding. She slipped again and cried out.

Flynn, responding to her distress, scooped her up in his arms and carried her the last few metres, ignoring her protests. He set her down gently on the back verandah of the old homestead. They were both plastered in mud. Prudence, her thin pink shirt moulded to her shivering body, was trying to stop her teeth from rattling against each other.

'We're home, sweetheart,' said Flynn, kissing her muddy forehead. 'And what you need first is a long, hot shower. Then we'll see to your injuries and get you into bed. You must be all in.'

Pru had no argument with that. She was far too exhausted.

'I'll dig you out some of my clothes,' said Flynn, guiding her towards the bathroom. 'Though I do have one item of yours.'

'You do?'

'Your purple sarong.' He winked. 'I brought it back with me from Bali, as a reminder of my one night with an attractive stranger with a crazy, exotic name.'

Pru caught sight of her mud-caked self in the bathroom mirror and gave a self-deprecating grin. 'Well, haven't we come a long way since then!' she said.

'You still look adorable to me, if a little muddy. Have your shower and I'll leave the clothes on the bed.'

The shower was a lifesaver. She then rubbed antiseptic lotion on her cuts and stuck plasters on those still bleeding before tumbling into bed, wearing nothing but a huge white T-shirt of Flynn's. She buried herself under the crisp clean covers so she couldn't hear the tempestuous storm raging outside. She tried to stay awake for Flynn's return, but fell into the deep, deep dreamless sleep of exhaustion.

It was pitch black when Pru awoke. Rain was still lashing down, the wind was still howling. She lay in the big bed and strained to hear something more than the storm hammering on the tin roof. Where was Flynn?

She stretched and then grimaced. Every bone and muscle ached like billy-o. She was sure she couldn't have

317

felt any worse if a bulldozer had run over her.

'Flynn?' She eased herself up on her elbows and tried to pierce the dark with her eyes. She was tempted to get up and try and find him. It was spooky; lying alone in a strange bed while the storm beat its relentless tattoo. 'Flynn?' she called again, louder this time.

A soft glow appeared through what must have been the open doorway. It got stronger as footsteps approached. Flynn then stood there with a hurricane lamp in one hand. In the muted light, Pru could see that he was wearing only dark boxer shorts. The rest of his body was thrown into light planes and mysterious shadows by the lamp's glow. He looked every bit like an ancient Greek god, golden and beautiful. Just as she'd thought in Bali, all those weeks ago.

Pru's mouth went dry. Suddenly she wished she hadn't called out for him but had lain silent, waiting patiently for the morning. She wasn't ready for

. . . for . . . this, whatever this was! She made a muffled, involuntary squawk.

'You okay, hon? I heard you call?' Flynn's voice was sleep husky and low. It was enough to make Pru's skin goosebump all over.

'Fine. I'm just fine. You go back to bed. I'm sorry if I woke you.'

'Hey, no sweat. I always sleep lightly through storms. How are you feeling?' He moved towards her and put the lamp on the bedside cabinet so they were bathed in the same lustrous pool.

How was she feeling? Where should she start? Anyway, she couldn't answer him because her throat had dried at his proximity. All her senses were alive and clamouring. She could smell his male-ness, the muskiness of his skin, and see the golden hairs glinting on his body in the lamplight. She was mesmerised, lost in a spell of her own weaving. Now it wasn't just the thumping of the rain on the roof filling her ears, but the thump of her heart as liquid fire flowed through her like a river.

'Pru?' He sat on the bed and reached out his hand to smooth it over her fuzzy scalp. She shivered at his touch. 'Do you have a fever?' he asked with concern and felt her forehead.

'No.'

'You feel hot.'

Hardly surprising with him sitting on her bed mostly naked!

She decided to change the subject. 'Why the lamp? Is this part of your Florence Nightingale act?'

'The lighting plant must have got damaged by the storm. All the electrics are out. Once the storm abates I'll go and check what's happened.'

He touched her cheek and smiled down at her, which again did nothing for her erratic heart rate.

'You don't know how sweet it is to have you finally lying in my bed,' he murmured.

'This is your bed?' Now why wasn't she surprised he hadn't put her in the spare bed?

'Oh yes! How does it feel, Amaryllis?

Does it meet with your approval?'

She couldn't resist a wiggle under the duvet. 'It's pretty comfortable.'

His eyes darkened. 'Like me to come in too, to check it out?'

Whoosh! There went her oxygen levels. Stars flashed behind her eyes and she felt all light-headed.

'It's a little chilly sitting here,' his voice dropped a couple of octaves.

So did Pru's breathing.

'Okay,' she whispered.

He lifted the covers and rolled in next to her. His body was indeed cold. Hers was hot. Fireworks sparked in all directions as their bodies touched and in panic, Pru tried to wiggle some distance between them.

Whew! That was better. But she inwardly cringed at her ineptness. She was no smooth operator. She was gauche and clumsy and totally inexperienced.

'I'm not going to bite.' Flynn's amusement lapped around her.

'I should hope not!' she said with tartness.

'Then come here.' His arms embraced her and he pulled her close. 'Warm me.'

'Okay . . . ' She wrinkled her nose as it tickled against his chest hair. If she kept him talking, everything would be all right, now wouldn't it?

Wrong!

'Kiss me . . . '

'Oh. Really?'

'Yes, really, Prudence.'

So she did.

'Gosh,' said Pru through passion-tingled lips a while later. Now both their bodies were hot but at least she felt a lot more relaxed in the circle of his arms, as if the first barriers of her inexperience had been broken down, as if she were almost home.

'Now show me your tattoo,' Flynn said with a hint of laughter.

Pru nibbled her bottom lip. Was she brave enough? Wasn't this the sort of occasion that Toni had talked about? They weren't quite butt-naked, but they weren't far off.

'Okay.' She rolled on her tummy and hiked up the baggy T-shirt, exposing her bare derriere. Flynn peered at it in the gloom of the lamplight.

'Hey,' said Pru, embarrassed. 'Are you short-sighted or something? You don't have to get quite so close, you know.'

He chuckled and gave the heart tattoo a loud, smacking kiss. 'Very cute. I feel humbled and honoured to think you've declared your feelings so intimately. Maybe I should get a corresponding one.'

Pru slapped him away and rolled back close. 'If you do, I insist on being there, especially if Toni is doing the tattooing.'

'Deal. Maybe it could be your present to me.'

'Why do you deserve a present, Maguire?'

'For my wedding. Our wedding . . . Marry me, Pru?'

She pulled away slightly, trying to view him in the lamplight, to gauge his expression.

'Are you serious?'

'Very.'

'But I didn't think you were big on marriage and commitment? What about all that stuff about how women couldn't be trusted, and endangering your precious station?'

'I've changed. You've changed me. Life at Ibis Springs would be pretty flat without you around, sweetheart. I'm willing to take the chance on love.' He kissed her again and then said, 'Are you?'

Pru lay in the circle of his arms and stared into the darkness beyond the pool of lamplight, as is she was searching for her answer.

'Prudence?'

'I think we've both done a lot of changing and growing these past weeks,' she said thoughtfully.

'So is that a yes? You'll marry me?'

'My idea of love has changed,' she carried on, as if she hadn't heard him.

'And?' He propped himself up on his elbow and stared intently at her.

'I thought I was in love with Dean for

years. But I think I was in love with the idea of love.'

'And?'

'Then I met you. And felt a whole swag of emotion I'd never realised I could feel.'

'I hope that's a good thing . . . ?'

'Yes, I think it is. I feel so much more alive since I met you. So yes, Flynn Maguire, I'll marry you.'

'Thank goodness for that. You had me worried for a moment.'

'Ah, but we do have some unfinished business from Bali.'

'We do?'

'Sampling a long, slow . . . '

Flynn interrupted her with a low and sexy laugh. 'I think that can be delivered. Come here, my not-so-prudent-Prudence and we'll see what we can do . . . '

THE END

THE FERRYBOAT

Kate Blackadder

When Judy and Tom Jeffrey are asked by their daughter Holly and her Scottish chef husband Corin if they will join them in buying the Ferryboat Hotel in the West Highlands, they take the plunge and move north. The rundown hotel needs much expensive upgrading, and what with local opposition to some of their plans — and worrying about their younger daughter, left down south with her flighty grandma — Judy begins to wonder if they've made a terrible mistake . . .

MEET ME AT MIDNIGHT

Gael Morrison

Nate Robbins needs the money bequeathed to him by his eccentric uncle — but in order to get it he must remarry before his thirtieth birthday, three weeks away. Deserted by her husband, Samantha Feldon is determined not to marry again unless she's sure the love she finds is true. So when her boss — Nate Robbins — offers her the job of 'wife', she refuses, but agrees to help him find someone suitable. Accompanying him on a Caribbean cruise, Sam finds him the perfect woman — realizing too late she loves Nate herself . . .

LOOKING FOR LAURIE

Beth James

On finding a dead body in her flat, Laurie Kendal fights her instinct to scream, and instead races to the nearest police station. About to embark upon a cycling holiday, DI Tom Jessop attends the scene, only to find . . . nothing! The body has inexplicably disappeared, and so he dismisses Laurie's story as rubbish. But there is something intriguing about Laurie — she is beautifully eccentric, yet vulnerable too, and earnest in her insistence that her story is true. So before starting his holiday, Tom has one more check on her flat . . .

A CHRISTMAS ENGAGEMENT

Jill Barry

Adjusting to life without her late husband, Molly Reid is determined to make the most of a holiday to Madeira. As the dreamlike days of surf and sun pass, a friendship with her tour guide Michael develops and grows, though she wonders whether his attention and care are just part of his job. Back in Wales, meanwhile, Molly's daughter and son-in-law are hatching a surprise family reunion over Christmas — and it looks like the family could be about to gain some new members . . .